The Way of Dharma

By Paul Twitchell

DHARMA dhahr'-mah *The law of life; the righteousness of life; doing what is right; the code of conduct that sustains the right ethics in life.*

Paul Twitchell
ECKANKAR DICTIONARY

THE WAY OF DHARMA

by Paul Twitchell

Copyright © 1970 ECKANKAR

All rights reserved. No part of this book may be reproduced, stored in a retrieval system, or transmitted in any form by any means, whether electronic, mechanical, photocopying, recording, or otherwise, without prior written permission of the copyright holder.

The terms ECKANKAR, ECK, EK, SOUL TRAVEL, and VAIRAGI, among others, are trademarks of ECKANKAR, P.O. Box 3100, Menlo Park, California 94026 U.S.A.

Printed in U.S.A.
ISBN: 0-914766-18-x
Eighth printing 1985

Cover painting by Diana Stanley

ECKANKAR
P.O. Box 3100, Menlo Park, CA 94026 U.S.A.

To all ECK Chelas
everywhere

THE WAY OF DHARMA
by
Paul Twitchell

CHAPTER 1

Captain Harvey Dodds, flight surgeon, U.S. Air Force, plodded wearily along the dusty road. His emaciated body was racked with an awful cough. Each footstep was a painful effort.

With extreme trouble he lifted his head and gauged the remaining distance to the Kazakhs' camp. He wondered if his legs would hold out or was it to be a rendezvous with death on this road lined by tall poplars? His tired gray eyes, sunk deep, in a thin face, saw the tree boughs swaying in a wind that swept down from the mighty snow-capped Himalayas.

Death was with him but Dodds was used to this grim spectre whose companionship he had shared these last two years. His clothes were a mass of tattered rags drooping from a wasted frame. Not a stitch was akin to his once natty Air Force uniform. Even his feet were wrapped in rags and skins. The Chinese prison had taken a toll of his health.

He had expected a reply from the American Ambassador at New Delhi, to a telegram sent yesterday, from Srinagar. Returning to the camp from Srinagar, he was disappointed. He applied to the city authorities for permission to stay in India until his country could make arrangements for return to the States.

Bhola Lal Ghosh, Mayor, said he was not sure what to do with Dodds. The decision rested entirely with the government. Captain Dodds was an escaped prisoner from China. Complications would arise between the United States and India if China demanded Dodds' return.

The Indian official, with long training in religion, looked upon this fever-racked American with compassion. He asked if Dodds would stay at his home until something could be learned. Dodds accepted, but asked permission to spend the night at the Kazakhs' camp. He wanted to bid farewell to those who saved his life.

Two years ago he was shot down over North Korea during a combat training flight while testing flyers' reactions for an experiment. He was captured and spent a year in a filthy prison camp in western China, tortured beyond belief, with lack of proper food, constant beatings and brainwashing.

Slowly he had built up plans for escape. One night he got past the sentry and fled westward toward Sinkiang, where almost at death's door he was found by a wild, nomad tribe of Kazakhs moving toward India in their flight from restrictions that Red China imposed on their native province. Upon arrival at the outskirts of Srinagar, a few days previously, only three hundred and fifty members of the tribe were left out of the original four thousand who started on their flight to freedom.

The dogs barked noisily at Harvey Dodds as he entered camp, clutching a small package of food under his left arm. Small, swarthy children glanced up laughingly from play as though the long, dark months and weary march so recently endured had already been forgotten. He walked on in deep fatigue toward the tent of the Chief, Tien Batir, passing many tribesmen who greeted him warmly.

Stopping before a broad tent of skins he called, and a low voice bade him enter. He found the weathered, old chieftain resting on a rug in the semi-darkness.

The old man stirred and spoke. "Your face tells me that there is no news from your countrymen in New Delhi?"

"None," Dodds replied seating himself on another rug. "The delay is unusual. The Mayor says that I can stay here tonight, but must go to the city tomorrow, to be his guest until what is decided to do with me. A policeman will be here all night to guard me. They think I might try to escape!"

He looked through the curtain opening. The encampment sat in a meadow by a crystal stream surrounded by fir-clad mountains, rising precipices and far above, the jagged snow-streaked Himalayas.

"My friend," said Tien Batir softly. "This is the laughter of the SUGMAD! You need not be watched. Where can you escape to this time?"

Harvey Dodds smiled. The haunted expression on his wasted countenance softened. "I've brought you some food," he said, opening the package.

He studied the canned beef and other tins hungrily. Selfishness worked like fury in his brain. But these were his friends and what he received, no matter how little it might be, would have to be divided with them.

"I praise your kindness, my son," said the old chief, his eyes glistening in the shadows. "Be not discouraged, the *SUGMAD will take care of ITS children. You are one of us no matter where you might be in this world!

"Take the food yourself. You need it worse than we do. You are too close to death for us to accept your gift!"

Dodds shook his head stubbornly.

Tien Batir smiled. "Very well. Come tonight and share it with my family. It will be the last time we shall see one another. If you live, then you will soon be in your land among your people. I will be in my grave!

"You are a good man," he continued. "In this land you will learn things that are beyond your beliefs. Before you return to America there are many surprises in store for you!"

"I will be here at sundown," Harvey said rising and bowing.

* Name of Supreme Being for followers of ECKANKAR, Ancient Science of Soul Travel.

He left the tent and moved along a lane of felt tents wondering if his strength would hold out until he could get proper medical care. The tribe's people did not respond to his greetings with the usual friendly, smiling laughter.

A small boy walked out of the throng and pulled at his sleeve. "A very beautiful lady is in your tent, Captain," he shrilled. "My father says it is wrong to have a woman in your tent if she is not your wife!"

"Did you say a woman?" He stared at the boy. "I know nobody here. None of the women of the tribe would be in my tent."

The boy replied, "She came from the city while you were at the tent of Tien Batir. She asked that I direct her to your tent. She is Hindu!"

A saddled mare with brown and white markings grazed near the tent. Curiosity burned hard in him making his tired body move rapidly toward the tent and leaving the boy behind. His heart beat with excitement.

He opened the flaps and stepped inside and his heart skipped a couple of beats. A woman was sitting in the rude chair he had found upon arrival at Srinagar. His first luxury in two years.

Her dark splendid eyes lifted to meet him. The boy was right for she was beautiful. Clad in a bright orange blouse and dark skirt, she rose gracefully from the chair with feline movements, greeting him in English.

Harvey Dodds stared intently at the lovely girl in his leaky old tent. Her hair, black as a raven's wing, glistened in the sunlight streaming through a ragged hole in his tent top.

He bowed low, heart pounding. For the first time in two years he had an opportunity to address a woman who was dressed in western attire and spoke English.

"I am Captain Harvey Dodds of the American Air Force," he said hoarsely, unable to keep his eyes off her loveliness.

She was about five feet four, with a dark, bronzed skin which glowed in the shadowy light. Her face was a sharply cut mold like an exquisite gem carved in relief and she had a small mouth and deep set eyes that revealed some deep light within her.

"I have come to warn you, Captain Dodds," her voice was wonderfully clear like waters whirling over mossy stones in a brook bed.

He thought of the wide, sleepy creeks swollen with the spring rains gushing through the pretty countryside and the great muddy river. Would he see Four Rivers again, or have the intimate warm feeling of seeing the sunlight play across the windows of the street?

"Who are you?" he asked.

"Amiya Ghosh!" Her fine dark eyes were suddenly veiled with shadows. "Daughter of Bhola Lal Ghosh, Mayor of Srinagar. He cannot do what is best for your interest. Others control him and the government of our province. They are powerful and influential. They would send you back to China!"

Fear swept through him. He stared at her as a silence ran between them. Sounds of the mare munching grass flowed into the tent. Death seemed to enter his brain and whisper for him to surrender.

The Mayor had said the power of granting Harvey Dodds' stay in Kashmir lay in the hands of the Governor of the Province. So that was it! The Communists had control here because they could threaten the frontiers of India with invasion unless their wishes were complied with.

"Why should I believe you?" he demanded more angry at himself than at her presence in his tent which meant a great insult to the Kazakhs.

"Trust me, Captain," she said in a rippling voice. "I have come to you risking great danger for my father. If the Communists learned of this they would cause trouble for my family!"

Anger made him speak. "You have caused me a great deal of embarrassment with my friends who helped me escape from the Chinese," he said. "The Kazakhs have a strict moral code about a bachelor having an unmarried woman in his tent. I do not wish to risk offending their friendship to hear what might be nonsense!"

"I have come in complete faith," she replied, calmly ignoring his words. Her voice had the sound of winds in the pine. "There are reasons why I have done this in disobedience of my family obligations. Do you realize that my visit here to a complete stranger is against the moral traditions of the Hindus?"

She continued. "I have a supreme purpose

in doing this, Captain Dodds. There are things beyond the ken of human thought. But I hope that you will relax your mind briefly enough to accept a small token of insight into the Will of God which I can reveal to you!"

He studied his long, thin hands which had almost become mutilated from the torture rack. They were still the hands of a surgeon. "I will try," he said. "Go ahead!"

She put a hand on his arm causing a deep thrill to course through his fatigued body. She said, "Our lives have been linked together throughout eternity. We have been together through many incarnations of physical life here on earth! And by this very fact I am compelled by God to help you escape from India, and return to your beloved country across the seas. You have a great destiny to fulfill in this world, Captain Dodds!"

He grinned at her intensity. "Very interesting, indeed, Miss Ghosh! A very lovely fairy tale. But tell me what plot is being hatched against me?"

Her eyes grew cloudy with hurt. "Well," she said hesitantly, "every communication with the proper authorities, including your American Ambassador, has been delayed for forty-eight hours until the Indian friends of the Chinese Reds have an opportunity to seize you and return you to the border where you will be cast back into prison again!"

Deep fears erupted within him like the sudden explosion of a violence spewing fire. "Is that why I haven't heard from the American Ambassador?" he cried.

"Your telegram was never sent," she replied calmly. "Other than father and the members of the city government nobody officially knows that you have escaped the Chinese and are now in this country!"

He thought of the little city, in America, where he was born, lying beside the waters of the great river. "What shall I do?" A groan escaped his lips. The giddy sickness was making his head swirl. "Where shall I go?"

She stepped closely to him with a quickness of an animal and laid both hands against his breast and looked into his face with an eager, intensive gaze. "Come quickly with me," she whispered fiercely. "I will show you the way to New Delhi where your Ambassador can give you the proper medical care and protection!"

He hesitated but she drove him into action with sharp words. "You cannot take time to decide, Captain Dodds. We must hurry for Nath Dwark, leader of the Kashmir Communists, already knows you are here and has sent his men to capture you!"

Harvey Dodds instantly propelled himself into action. He seized his duffle bag and stuffed his meager belongings into it. Finishing, he turned to the girl and looked at her, wondering if it were his emotions that gave him confidence in this beautiful Hindu girl, or was it his great desire for freedom?

He said, "I believe you and trust you. Where will you take me?"

"To the Chittava Ashram at Kumur where you will find the Living ECK Master, Swarachakraji. He will protect you from harm until you reach the proper authorities!"

Captain Harvey Dodds threw back the curtains and let the girl pass and then stepped into the sunlight. A crowd of the Kazakhs had gathered around the tent awaiting him. There was an aura of bewilderment in their countenances that struck him instantly of their wonder at his actions. He realized what their attitudes might be. These kindly people of the steppes were not hostile but aghast at his breach of their moral code in allowing a woman to remain at any length of time in his tent. They were aware that something was amiss and expected an explanation.

Turning to Amiya Ghosh, he said, "I must see Tien Batir, Chief of the tribe, and explain why you are here. He expects me for a farewell dinner tonight. He has been my friend for these many months and I cannot express my gratitude too greatly for his trouble in helping me escape the enemy."

The girl shook her dark, lovely head. "I am sorry, Captain Dodds, but we do not have time. Every moment is precious to us. Come, let us leave here now!"

"Then let me send a message to Tien Batir," he replied, swiftly motioning for the same lad who had given him the message that Amiya Ghosh was awaiting him.

Harvey Dodds started to speak but the stoic silence of the Kazakhs was suddenly broken by a murmur of voices at the edge of the crowd. A tug at his sleeve made him turn around to find Amiya Ghosh pointing at two strange horsemen entering the west side of the camp.

Her voice was lifted with sharp alarm. "They are Nath Dwark's men!" she cried. "The one wearing the tall hat is Rosha, the killer. Come, we must hurry and escape them or all is lost. My mount is there. Quickly, let us both mount and get to the city. There we will be safe in my father's house!"

Wheeling around, Captain Harvey Dodds faced the crowd and spoke rapidly in the hoarse Kazakh dialect while pointing at the two strangers on horseback, nearing the edge of the encampment. He told them why Amiya Ghosh had come to his tent and stayed there and the warning that she had brought for him to leave the camp at once.

He said that the strangers were the sons of the Red Dogs who had driven the Kazakhs from their great motherland of the steppes. Now he and the girl needed their help to escape from the Red Dogs riding down on the camp to seize them.

A low murmuring growl arose from the crowd. They understood what the words Red Dogs meant, and were ready to defend their great American friend, Captain Harvey Dodds, of the United States Air Force, who had almost rotted in the Chinese prison.

A short, stocky nomad, with a fuzzy beard, wearing a tall, velvet hat, leaped out of the crowd and gave a terse order.

He signalled for the Kazakhs to follow and in a body they marched out to meet the strangers, and blocked their entrance into the camp. In the confusion, Amiya Ghosh and Dodds mounted the little mare and swiftly galloped it out of the farther side of the encampment.

The horse moved rapidly across the flower decked meadow where the vivid blue sky was a vast milky dome stretching from each mountain range to the other. They came into the suburban area of the city at a fast gallop, scattering children from the dusty streets. A dog dashed out from between the houses and tried to nip the mare's shanks. The mount jerked backward snorting, but the girl got it under control again and turned into a short, narrow street.

Presently they came to a flat white house that had ornate, grilled windows and doors. The mare pranced into the courtyard where clucking hens marched around the yard and a white Brahma cow stood placidly chewing her cud. A small stone altar shimmered in the sunlight and heat reflected from the building.

A very old, wrinkled servant in a long, brown robe, arose from the porch and hobbled forward, looking as though he was a part of the ancient brick wall surrounding the courtyard. He took the mare's reins as they dismounted.

The girl motioned for Captain Harvey Dodds to follow her and led the way through an archway into an inner court, then entered the house through a series of iron-wrought gates. Inside was dark and cool with a feeling of mysterious aura as she stepped across the threshold into a broad room which was apparently a library, for the walls were lined with books that had titles in many different languages. The room was designed in mahogany paneling and furniture with leather chairs in customary English styling.

Dodds looked up as he entered and gave a start, for a tall, thin man with iron gray hair, and dressed in a white robe, got up from a chair. Surprise was written across his long, lantern countenance. It was the Mayor of Srinagar.

Amiya Ghosh walked toward her father with her hips moving in a slow natural sway and gently kissed his cheek. Turning to Harvey Dodds, she said gently. "This is my father, Bhola Lal Ghosh. You met him today in his office, at the Municipal Center."

Then she turned and spoke rapidly to her father in Hindustani. The tall man looked up at Captain Dodds with dark, compassionate eyes. He moved forward with his hand outstretched. "Welcome to our humble home, Captain Dodds!" His English was flawless and his voice was a solemn, round tone. "I bid you to sit and eat. I am just as surprised at this as yourself. My daughter's actions were unexpected. But please do not be embarrassed for now that you are here we will decide upon some action to help you!"

A sickly feeling stirred heavily in Harvey Dodds' stomach. Perspiration dotted his brow. He wiped it off with his hand as he sank into a deep, soft chair. Was he going

— 13 —

to be ill? That strange feeling of tightness around his chest made his heart beat faster. He could not seem to breathe. What was this queer feeling which gave him so much trouble? Suppose that it could have been his prison experience and that long march to freedom? His sojourn in a dark prison where his heart was always in his mouth might have been the cause of this. He fought against that creepy sensation which always made him feel as though he were going to faint.

"Your kindness is greatly appreciated, sir," he said hoarsely. "But I have nothing to offer you for your help!"

A brilliant smile crossed Lal Ghosh's lean face. "It is a great deal of pleasure to both of us to spoil any plot that Nath Dwark might have."

"But this will cause you trouble," Harvey Dodds said anxiously, while wiping the sweat off his brow.

"Not a bit," smiled Lal Ghosh moving toward the table in the center of the room and clapping his hands. He ordered food from the servant that appeared and turned back to Harvey Dodds who was looking pale and sickly. "I had no way of helping you while you were in my office previously, because the clerk who was taking dictation is a Communist agent. The best I could do was to promise you a little in the way of hospitality. Now that my daughter was fortunate to be in meditation and caught a vision of the danger you were in, and did the work which I anticipated doing, in a less bombastic manner, we will proceed from here!"

Something deep down inside Captain Dodds began stirring around like an old witch's brew in a cauldron. The feeling nauseated him and his head started spinning. His heart pounded as though it would fall out of his breast.

"I'm sorry!" he said faintly. "But I am sick!"

He looked at his host and the girl. Their faces seemed to waver. Closing his eyes he opened them and looked again. This time it was worse. Suddenly he seemed to be sliding down a long tunnel into a deep pit of inky blackness.

Bhola Lal Ghosh sat at the table, in the library of his home, that evening with his daughter and son. They were his pride and joy, the hope of his life. He considered Shyama, his son, his right hand and Amiya, his left. His wife, who had gone to bed early because of a headache, was his heart. They were the aspects of the great Reality manifested on earth to give him the beauty and joy of living.

Would it be possible that they could carry out the divine mission which had been entrusted to him? He let the thought run through his mind as he studied their youthful faces in the lamp light. The possession of the sacred scroll of the great ECK Saint, Fubbi Quantz, written possibly in the year of 1418 A.D., was an honor beyond comprehension, but most dangerous. He had to find a way to get it to the Master at the Chittava Ashram, Kumur.

He had planned that the safest and simplest method was to let Shyama carry the scroll to the Living ECK Master, Swarachakraji. Nobody would suspect a boy of seventeen to be carrying such a valuable manuscript but would look at him in the light of a youthful pilgrim going to worship with the living Master.

There were complications standing in the way of this plan. Bhola Lal Ghosh believed that Nath Dwark knew about the scroll which was supposed to have been taken down in Sanskrit from the original copy of Fubbi Quantz's magnificent collection of poems called *The Way*.

If Dwark decided to seize the ancient, priceless relic, there would be great danger to face for the scroll was supposedly worth a fortune to whoever possessed it. Something had to be worked out so that the Master could get it into his hands. It would be safe with him until ready to be shipped to America or England for final inspection and sale.

Lal Ghosh had purchased the manuscript from a shepherd boy who had found it in a cavern in the foothills of the Himalaya mountains. There were certain dangers in letting it become known to the public as to what the contents of the manuscript contained. Now with the American on his hands, Lal Ghosh was a little puzzled as to what to do.

"I don't exactly know what to do with the American officer," Lal Ghosh said voicing his fears to his children. "I can't inform the American authorities that he is here for then the Kashmir Government would reprimand me for going over their heads. Meanwhile, he must be put somewhere so nobody will know where he is and be in absolute safety!"

"Why couldn't I take him to the ashram with me?" asked Shyama, a slender, brown-eyed boy whose dark face seemed to gleam with an inward joyous light. He had long fingers and well-formed hands. "He would be perfectly safe there!"

His sister shook her head. "I do not believe it is true. He would never get there. His condition is so bad that he should not be moved from the house for several days!"

"I agree with my son," Bhola Lal Ghosh said gently looking at his daughter tenderly. "The ashram is the only place where he will be safe. It is dangerous for us as long as he is in this house. Nobody except the Master can protect him while he is in India, not even the government officials will disobey the Master's wishes!"

He continued, "Captain Dodds will never suspect that Shyama is secretly carrying the ancient scroll of our ancient Saint to the ashram for safe keeping until we can get it out of the country!"

Amiya said anxiously. "But the American

officer will be a burden on my brother. He is sick and the Reds will be watching for him. They might seize Shyama and find the manuscript on him!"

"I realize the added dangers," replied Bhola Lal Ghosh seriously. "Perhaps we can put them in the proper disguise which will get both through to the ashram safely.

"They can go dressed like pilgrims and the Captain can play the part of a sick, old man, who is deaf and dumb, fulfilling his long life's ambition to see the ECK Master Swarachakraji. I will provide the necessary funds but you, my son, must beg for food and make your role more realistic. Every precaution must be taken for your lives depend upon your ability to play the game."

"I can be a good, and brave actor, my father," said the boy smiling while his eyes glistened with the prospects of adventure on the open road of India.

"Do you know the dangers, my son?" asked Bhola Lal Ghosh seriously. "The manuscript is one of the most ancient in the world and is of great value to anyone. Fortunately, we hope that nobody knows about it but the ones intimately concerned, for when I purchased it for only a rupee from that old ignorant shepherd it was thought to be only a piece of old sheepskin dug out of an old vase in the foothills. But my friend Professor Vyasa, at the University, has said that it was one of the rare treasures of the world. Without doubt it is the first copy of the ECK poem collection called *The Bytag*. It could be the original, and who knows?"

Amiya asked abruptly, "Don't you think that we could send it by guard express, Father?"

"No. That would attract the attention of the newspapers and we would have too much publicity on it. I do not wish to announce it until we have it safely in a place in England or America. There will be a great deal of money paid for the scroll by a foreign museum!"

The door opened and a stocky man wearing a white turban came into the room. He carried a physician's handbag. "Ha, Doctor," called Bhola Lal Ghosh. "How is the patient? Is he better?"

The stocky, little man shook his head sadly. "I am very, very sorry, my good friends, but the man is extremely close to death. He needs food and long rest. A real, long rest. Not just a week in bed, but months. Unless he has these I cannot tell how long that he will last. Maybe a day, or maybe a week!"

"For the purpose of safety I must remove him to Kumur. Will it be possible?"

The physician shook his head most fiercely. "I repeat that the man is sick. He is a living corpse. However, it does not matter where he dies. Here in your house or at Kumur, if he gets there. But do as you please, my dear friend!"

Bhola Lal Ghosh put his hand on the physician's shoulders and gazed steadily into the man's eyes. "I must have your promise not to reveal the identity of my guest, Doctor Mukerjee? It is not safe for me to have him here!"

"I do not discuss my patients with anyone," replied the physician gruffly shaking off Ghosh's hand. "But should anybody get curious I will respect your desire and not repeat what was seen here. I shall tell them that it was a call for your wife!"

"Thank you, Doctor Mukerjee!" Ghosh called after the little doctor who was hustled out of the door.

Turning to his family, he said. "We will plan for Shyama and the American officer to leave tomorrow morning early!"

CHAPTER 2

Lucia Whitfield gazed through her hotel window at the sun drenched city of New Delhi. Life was stirring in the streets below, in an early morning pageantry. Tiny Indian women, in flowing robes, strolled through the streets with market baskets under their arms.

Lucia was exceedingly slender. She had a heart-shaped face with dark skin and freckles sprinkled over a snubbed nose. Her mouth was long and pulpy and her eyes a gleaming hazel. Turning, she went back into the closet and selected a yellow dress.

She had arrived there, from New York, the day before, with her father. She was the only child of the family and her mother, long deceased, left her to be a traveling companion for her father on many business trips.

She decided to go downstairs and await her father's return from the American Embassy where he had gone on business for the Gatewood Chemical Corporation, of which he was president.

In the lobby she took the first comfortable chair. Suddenly, she thought of Harvey Dodds. She remembered him as a long, lanky boy who had become a well-known surgeon in her home town, Four Rivers. A hatred existed between their families. His father, a physician, supposedly gave Lucia's mother a prescription that killed her, after Lucia's birth. Harvey had been shot down during the Korean War, by enemy planes, and reported dead.

Looking up suddenly she found a strong looking man in a short maroon robe, standing there. He had coal black eyes and short clipped hair. The beard that covered his face was closely clipped. He looked like a medieval monk.

"Miss Whitfield?" he said in precise English.

"Yes?" she asked, wondering who this was.

"I have a message for you."

"Yes, what is it?" she said impatiently.

"You wonder at your urge to come to India." He smiled faintly. "The great mystery of God is ready to be revealed to you. But only the Living ECK Master can give you this secret. Go to his ashram and learn the secret there. You will find a fellow American, Captain Dodds!"

She gasped as he looked at her with very wise, old eyes and continued. "You were thinking of him, my lady. He is there with the Master, but in great danger. You can help if you will listen to the great Master!

"Your life has been spent in seeking. Seek, seek, my lady and never be without hope for there is greatness in the glory of God. The living Guru, Swarachakraji, can give you the path to reach that glory!"

He left suddenly going through the door in strong stride on sandaled feet. She stared at the empty doorway, her thoughts driving hard against the screen of her mind.

Rising she went across to the desk. "Who

was the man who just spoke to me?" she asked the clerk.

"Man?" the clerk said curiously. "I didn't see anyone talking with you, Miss Whitfield. I saw you there alone and presumed you were asleep!"

"Never mind. It was nothing," she said awkwardly.

Her father, R. J. Whitfield, a robust, broad-faced man, six feet and some two hundred pounds, came through the door in a vigorous stride. Dressed in white linens he carried a briefcase and cane. "Lucia!" he boomed. "Let's go into the lounge for coffee. I want to talk with you!"

They ordered drinks in the dimly lighted room. R. J. spoke loudly, his rugged face beaming. "I'm going to get that site at Allahabad. Make a good location for a plant in that part of India!"

He frowned quickly. "Heard something curious over at the Embassy. Remember Harvey Dodds? He was killed in Korea, but they told me that a mysterious message had been received about him being in India."

She gripped the table edge. "What is it, Father?"

"The thing is incoherent. The Ambassador doesn't understand. Somebody is in India who apparently thinks he's Harvey Dodds. They're investigating but think it's a rumor. It'd be too bad if Dodds was resurrected!"

The long white road was a ribbon under the hot sun, winding through a green jungle toward dim mountains. Harvey Dodds, disguised in a white pilgrim robe and cowl, rode a small donkey, wearily led by Shyama.

Dodds was desperately sick. He could hardly think of anything but that pain in his body. Occasionally visions of his hometown, lying at the mouth of the Tennessee River, which emptied into the muddy Ohio before the town's levee, crossed his mind.

They were trying to reach Lahore in the Punjab Province where they could board an express train for Kumur. Dodds did not believe he would survive the journey.

He had been pulled out of a sickbed, filled with narcotics, and put on the donkey. He groaned with every step the beast took. The rocking motion kept his stomach stirred up until he was constantly nauseated.

They had traveled for three days and nights resting little on the side of the highway which was filled with pilgrims enroute to the Kumba Mela, the spiritual festival held every twelve years, at Allahabad. But Dodds hardly knew anything that was happening.

They came to a small wooded glade, on the third evening, where Dodds fell from the beast and staggered up the embankment to drop on the grass wondering if this was the end. His thoughts were on Amiya, her warmth and loveliness.

Shyama got water and made him swallow a pill, then cooked some food. Dodds had grown fond of the Hindu lad and began calling him Sammy. Shyama seemed to like the American version.

Dodds tried to sleep but suddenly opened his eyes to find a strong looking man with burning black eyes standing nearby. The man said in a deep voice. "Do you seek liberation, my sons?"

Shyama interrupted. "My brother cannot speak, nor hear, seeker of truth. He is old and sick!"

A strange light beamed in the dark eyes. "Perhaps you will tell him that I will give the future of this good Soul?"

"Why does he need to know the future?"

"I tell the tall, sick one what lies ahead. A good deed is repaid with a good deed— a bad deed with a bad one. Does not the great Yaubl Sacabi say this?"

Shyama signalled Dodds to give the man his attention. The man squatted. "My dear ones, you travel to the deathless Swarachakraji. Beware for there are the evil ones who seek you. They now seek you over the countryside, among the pilgrims. They watch the airports and the railway stations.

"Life will stay with you, be not afraid of this. I advise that you not go to Kumur, for the Wheel of Heaven is at Allahabad attending the Kumba Mela. Go there instead, for you will see the blessed one, Viswapati, Lord of the World.

"Watch for the girl from the foreign land. She seeks you here in India!"

He disappeared suddenly along the road

in the deep cloud of dust raised by the marching feet of the pilgrims.

Groaning, Dodds got up. "Let us leave quickly. That was an enemy agent."

"That must have been Rebazar Tarzs, the great ECK Master," replied the boy. "But let us travel for a while among the pilgrims. I believe it will be safer in the crowd!"

They went on until completely exhausted, then lay down again on the roadside. Dodds told the boy to sleep while he watched, but soon dozed off himself.

Almost instantly he awoke with a feeling of danger. Fear swooped through him like a gale at sea, for reared over the sleeping boy was a great snake with its head spread wickedly to strike.

Slowly he rose reaching for a stick of wood and moved a step at a time circling behind the weaving serpent. Then he struck with hard, fast blows. The thrashing of the snake awoke the boy who leaped out of its way. Dodds dropped the stick and seized a stone and pummeled the serpent.

Shyama looked at the dead serpent fearfully. "It is a cobra," he said tremblingly. "I don't know how you killed it for cobras never allow anyone to get close enough to strike them with a stick!"

Dodds sat down silently with his face in his hands.

Shyama moved to his side. "I am in debt to you until a good deed can rectify it. My will is your will to do whatever you wish with me!"

Dodds laughed hollowly. "It is I who am

in debt to you and your family. Let us leave this awful place!"

"Wait a minute," said the boy putting a hand on Dodd's shoulder. "I must tell you something. It is only fair to you!"

Dodds looked at him inquiringly.

"You have been misled. My whole famliy fortune is tied up in this journey. My father did not tell you all!"

Dodds was startled. "I thought this trip was to help me?"

"Father planned for me to take an ancient scroll to the Master for safekeeping. You arrived about the time I was to leave and it was decided that you be taken along to the ashram!"

"What do you mean, Sammy?" Dodds was bewildered.

"The scroll which I am carrying is possibly the original copy of a collection of poems called "The Way," written about the year 1418 by one of the earlier Saints of my spiritual teaching, ECKANKAR, Ancient Science of Soul Travel. Father got it from a shepherd who found it in a vase in a mountain cave. An antiquarian said it might be the original.

"Father believes the Master will take care of it until you are ready to leave the country, and we might be able to talk you into taking it to America for sale to a museum. If it were known that we had the scroll, murder might be attempted to seize it!"

A cool wind blew up driving away some of the heat. Shyama felt a shiver run up his spine as though his intuition was telling him it was wrong to tell Captain Dodds about the manuscript.

After a while Dodds said, "Who is this Fubbi Quantz?"

"He is a saint, philosopher and poet of great renown. He lives in northern Tibet. From his birth he was known to be a Saint sent to this earth for helping all mankind. He has written many beautiful works which are known in the West."

Harvey Dodds said, "Your family is a follower of this spiritual teaching, you just mentioned. What does it mean?"

The boy's black eyes were fixed in a steady gaze on Dodds. "I believe you are serious. Too many ask only to argue and criticize. I do not wish to waste breath on the negative aspects of any beliefs."

Dodds said. "I am serious. There must be something deep under the surface of what one sees in India, like the yogis who push pins through their cheeks or sleep on iron spikes."

"Many do these things for it makes them an easy living. It is what you call in American slang, grandstanding.

"Some of them are what might be called spiritual drunkards. They are people caught on a low spiritual plane and can't go either way. It takes a great Master like Swarachakraji to help them. They are considered crazy people in your country.

"ECKANKAR is the most ancient of all spiritual teachings. It is the science of the cosmic sound current, that comes from the far dim beginning of time on earth, when

God manifested ITSELF into the world. The teachings are older than the Vedas which religious scholars consider the first spiritual teachings. My Master is a living Saint in the line of the tradition of the Ancient Order of Vairagi Masters.

"If you wish to enter into the Kingdom of God, as Fubbi Quantz calls this state, you must find the Living ECK Master who can open your Spiritual Eye so you can see the Light of God, and open your spiritual ears to hear the Voice of God. This Voice is the real living Master, so says my Guru."

Harvey Dodds said slowly. "So you believe in God!"

Shyama nodded. "ECKANKAR is the study of God's Voice. It is the very ancient path to heaven. But you must first find the living Master, a genuine Sat Guru, and be initiated by him. You will not make any real advancement on the path until this is done."

He turned away. "We must go. But our destination is Allahabad where we will find the Master."

"Allahabad?" Dodds said sharply. "It is foolish to go there. Perhaps your Master did not go there."

"The beggar said he was at Allahabad."

"The beggar could have been an enemy agent."

Shyama smiled. "But it was Rebazar Tarzs. The SUGMAD does things in a mysterious way."

"All the same I wish to continue to Kumur. I feel we will have protection there."

Shyama looked at the dead snake and shivered. "There is wisdom in your words!"

"I don't care if Dodds died in Korea or a Chinese prison camp," R. J. Whitfield said reading his paper in the hotel suite.

Lucia said annoyed. "You've had your revenge on his family. You drove Dr. Dodds out of practice. You've fought with Miss Carrie Dodds over that waterfront property for years. Your hatred has infected me but if Harvey is in India and alive we should help him."

Whitfield lighted a slim cigar. "I don't want to hear any more," he said savagely. "His death was good for all concerned."

"You were responsible for him being recalled to active duty in Korea?" she said with surprise.

His jaw tightened. "Hasn't this feud gone on for years? Hasn't old Carrie Dodds fought our Four Rivers' plant by putting her hand into the city affairs there? Her meddling has cost me plenty to maintain that plant." He cleared his voice. "We've got a two-million-dollar contract at that plant for the Navy on a sixty day work period. If she does anything to upset it, I'll bring suit against her."

"R. J.", she said in a husky voice, "I think it would be good if I go to Kumur and investigate that report on Harvey Dodds."

"What?" he shouted.

"Don't get excited. You know what the doctors say about your heart."

"Confound the doctors!" he roared. "They are all alike. Look what they did to your mother."

"There are other stories about my mother's death. You broke her heart over other women." She quickly changed the subject. "I hear that Harvey is in Kumur in an Indian ashram."

"I won't allow you to go!" he raged.

"It won't cost you anything," she flushed deeply. "I'll use my own money. By the way, you forgot to tell people when bragging about being a self-made man in the business world that you worked up from a clerk to president. You don't tell anybody you married the boss' daughter and her money put you where you are today. The only thing you ever did for me was to give me an independent income. That's more than I can say for you chasing every woman who shows up at the office, even Julie Vanners when she came up from Four Rivers several weeks ago. Oh, this is useless!"

"All right," he smothered his rage. "I'll get Murray Price, our plant supervisor here, to check on the story at Kumur. If it's Dodds, we can help without him knowing it. And by the way, Price is trying to get me interested in some local junk, supposed to be an ancient manuscript of an ancient Indian Saint. Says it's worth a fortune. But he hasn't produced it yet!"

A knock on the door interrupted him.

"That's Murray Price now. Let's look a little calmer please!"

Amiya Ghosh preened herself before a full-length mirror. A diamond cluster in her left nostril flashed as she put a bright orange scarf around her shoulders. She was dressing for a late afternoon tea-party in the neighborhood.

"I don't understand about Shyama," she said to her mother, a tiny woman, on a couch. "He has been gone a week. Somebody would have sent word about them."

"You've made no contact with him through Mauna?" asked the mother.

The girl pasted a tiny red patch on her broad forehead representing the spiritual eye of God and shook her head. This was strange for ordinarily she could contact her brother anywhere. They were both sensitives and mental telepathy was common to them.

Suddenly she faced her mother anxiously and said. "If the Kashmir Reds learn that Father and I are in the plot to help the American officer, they might try to kill father. Maybe with poison at an official dinner, or a dagger in the back or by bullet."

"Put your trust in the SUGMAD, my dear," her mother smiled. "If suffering comes it must be the will of God. Run along now and have a good time!"

A servant entered the room. "I have a message from your honorable parent! He desires your presence at his office at once!"

"Why didn't he use the telephone?" she said knowing something was wrong, but annoyed because she was perfectly dressed for the party and must leave now. "I will go. Perhaps it is something about my brother!"

She hurried away from the house aware that her action was too fast for that of a Hindu woman, but impatience drove her into a quicker step. She came to the market place crowded with a gay throng.

A dark, ugly man with a long white scar across his face blocked her path. "Someone wishes to speak with you!" his voice was hoarse.

She tried to pull away from his heavy hand that seized her and pulled her into a nearby door. Half stumbling, and crying with rage, she was flung into a small, dark, ill-smelling room.

R. J. Whitfield studied his strong features in the bathroom mirror. He imagined himself to be a living example of what a great captain of industry might be.

His indomitable will had carried him to the top of the industrial and financial world, to become president of the greatest corporation of its kind in the world. The city of Four Rivers intended to erect a huge stone statue of him, in one of its public parks. He had provided for the payment in his will.

He was irritated with Lucia for she kept harping that he should give his home town a new hospital. The tiny clinic there was always overflowing with patients especially from the Gatewood Plant.

He slid into his coat and went into the living room to call for the girl. She appeared in the doorway of her bedroom. "You have to shout?" she asked irritably.

He smiled tolerantly. She was like other women. None understood him except Elsa Spain, his secretary, who could anticipate his whims and desires. But she too had been getting a little too insolent since his affair with Julie Vanners, and was left home on this trip.

"I would like to take a trip to Kumur where the ashram of that religious teacher is located," she said stiffly.

"That sounds crazy, Lucia," he said, wondering at her. Frankly, he never knew her. The only thing of concern in his life was money. He took money seriously, not because he had great quantities of it himself, but because he was responsible for it. By constantly living in a world of money and money problems, he had come to think that the universe was co-ordinated principally through the monetary system. "I forbid you to do this. Your real reason is to find Harvey Dodds."

"Not exactly. But you wouldn't understand. However, I've had as much as I can take from you. When we get back to New York, I'm going to find myself an apartment to live alone. Mother left me enough money to get along on, and I've got some good stock in the Corporation. All right, that's said. Let's go to breakfast."

He laughed as they left the suite. "I've got some news for you which is better than running off after some ragged Hindu who is preaching that he is God and that you can be too!"

They walked to the elevator where he punched the button and turned to speak, wondering if he had a blind spot in his mental process approaching naiveness in his ability to overlook her rights and desires. "You need not chase off after one Indian Holy Man. With your wealth, talent, brains and social position you can have them come to you by the dozens and preach in your backyard."

"What do you mean?"

"I got word this morning to take a train to Allahabad tonight to look over that plant site for Gatewood. Plenty of water, cheap manpower and good transportation, they say."

"What's this got to do with me?" she asked.

"There is a spiritual conflab going on there, called the Kumba Mela. All the holy men of India gather there every twelve years to hold their convention on how to become God." He smiled. "Want to go?"

She nodded. "All right, if you don't object

to me trying to run down that rumor on Harvey Dodds."

He cleared his throat. "Better let Price handle that. I told him last night to do the job. He just telephoned a few minutes ago and said something about that old scroll belonging to that Indian Saint had been found."

Nath Dwark rode through the soft green hills, on his iron gray stallion, concerned about the whereabouts of the American Air Officer Dodds. If Dodds was not found soon, Dwark would be in trouble with the Reds.

The stallion climbed the ridge. Beyond Dwark lay the magnificent scene of valleys and mountains, each wave of the rising Himalayas a deeper and deeper purple as it shaded off toward the plains and upward to the great ranges with their glistening snowy summits rising closely above the trees.

Dwark inhaled the deep draughts of tingling air and rubbed the glossy stallion's neck. He was a huge, handsome man with a dark, rugged face and a hooked nose. His eyes were set wide and were jet black. His sweeping shoulders under the white shirt showed a physical stature which pronounced power.

Reddish cavalry boots peeped from under orange pantaloons. A brace of pistols were thrust in a purple cummerbund around a trim waist. A wicked knife was slung from a swinging shield. His nomadic appearance was completed by an embroidered vest and white turban.

He frowned, thinking about his problem of money which was needed badly to maintain his leadership of the provincial Reds. He was far too ambitious and his prospects were always bound up in himself and assumed cosmic proportions in either failure or success.

Far along the mountain trail a sentry from the camp challenged him. He rode onward until reaching the camp where ragged hillmen with bandoliers were playing cards, on the ground.

He dismounted and strode through, kicking money and cards off the blanket indifferent to their protests. Inside the cave sat Rosha, most reliable member of his gang, puffing a long cigarette and fiddling with a wireless set. The smokey torch made the cavern gloomy.

Dwark sat down on a wooden keg. "I got your message," he said shortly.

The white scar gleamed on Rosha's evil face. "The American named Price paid me to do a job for him yesterday. It fits into what you are searching for."

"What did the American have you do?"

"Kidnap the daughter of Lal Ghosh!" Rosha whispered.

"I had other plans." Dwark said harshly. "Why did you do it?"

Fear spread across Rosha's face. "Price thinks Lal Ghosh has that scroll of Fubbi

Quantz, 'The Way'!"

"What's that got to do with us?" Dwark lashed out.

"Lal Ghosh sent his son to the ashram at Kumur with the American officer for some reason other than what appears on the surface. Ghosh's son is carrying a manuscript supposed to be the original of 'The Way'. If he gets the American officer out of the country, the man would carry it to America where it can be sold for lots of rupees."

"Well?"

Rosha groveled in the dust. "Price had me kidnap the girl so he can learn where the manuscript is. Payment for her freedom is that scroll. He says his employer, the great American capitalist, R. J. Whitfield is interested and might pay cash now."

Dwark stood up suddenly. "Where's the girl?"

"In the other cave near the center of its heart. Price was here but gone now. I've a woman with her."

"Rosha," Nath Dwark stood straight looking at the cringing henchman. "This might be a master stroke. We won't let Price have the manuscript and we will be able to find out where that American officer is now. Take me to this woman!"

Captain Harvey Dodds and his young

companion reached Lahore, at dawn, a week following their departure from Srinagar. A large, noisy crowd surging through the streets mingled with the thousands of pilgrims, shouting, singing and laughing.

Dodds disposed of his mule by tying it to a post and walking away. He had to lean upon the Hindu lad's shoulder to keep his balance. His mind whirled in a dizzy pace. Every minute he thought this might be the end of the journey for himself.

He suggested that they join the crowd and move with it as closely as possible to the railroad station for it might keep from attracting the attention of anyone who was on the lookout for them.

Eventually, they reached the station where droves of pilgrims, in white robes, sat wearily on the platform awaiting the Allahabad Express. Shyama went to the ticket office and purchased a pair of tickets to Kumur.

Dodds leaned against a post munching on a banana which the boy brought back with him while thinking of the Indian girl's soft beauty, the gentle touch of her hand on his arm and the deep mystery in her eyes.

He wondered if he were in love with her. He was a Westerner and his normal life was altogether different from hers. Besides, if he reached the states, there would be plenty of opportunities for marriage. Yet she was different—she had spoken of a link between themselves when they met in the camp of the Kazakhs, and of his great destiny. He would speak to Shyama about this some day.

The arrival of the train disrupted his

thoughts and they boarded it to ride through the day. They reached their destination, the city of Kumur, late that night.

Shyama led the way across the city to the ashram. Electric lights gleamed upon the ruins of stones everywhere. He felt himself as he really was. Only skin and bones. A vibration reached out across the gulf of time and united him with this strange place.

The city was an ancient crossroads of the world in the early history of time. He had sat here, crosslegged beneath the trees, in another life watching the camel caravans arriving from China with loads of spice and goods. Here the great Hill King, Shivji broke the last stronghold of the Moguls, and Alexander, conqueror of the world, established court to listen to the Indian sages preach the eternity of God.

They reached the gates of the ashram. Walls loomed out of the night, under the street lights, that swung in a strong wind. All looked weird and repelling to Harvey Dodds. He stood there briefly, looking at them with sick eyes wondering if the Greek Alexander had stood in the same spot and witnessed what went on before his mind.

Was this a dream? He asked himself that question in the space of a moment. Could it be possible that this was his Soul body traveling in another world witnessing something that he could not possibly see with physical eyes? His heart pounded fast from the expectations of seeing the Master. Would the Master heal him as Shyama had promised?

A small man, in a brown robe, came forward to greet them. He put his hands together and bowed, answering in English. "The Master is not here. But I can take you to Jumnaji who is in charge while the Master is away. He is expecting you."

Dodds wondered at this. They had not sent word of their coming. Jumnaji, an Indian Master in his own rights, who chose to serve the Swarachakraji, was sitting crosslegged under a tree before a large fire. He was middle-aged, clean shaven, bald and naked save for a loincloth.

"We have been expecting you," he spoke in English joining his finger tips together in answer to Shyama's salutation. "The Master said you would be here at this hour."

Harvey Dodds murmured something and sat down wearily. He felt better, but wondered how the news had travelled so fast without communication by letter or telephone.

He knew there was little need to be in a hurry to discuss his problem for the Indian seemed to know what was in his mind. Time meant nothing to these people. Karma ruled them, to some extent, and their belief in God's will was infectious to Dodds. He felt neither hurried, nor eager, nor surprised; this seemed to have been planned before his birth. He needed only to sit and listen to what was told him and follow out the plans.

Shyama brought water and gave him two pills, then Dodds sat back and looked at the strange brown man sitting there with the firelight flickering on his body. This was

— 41 —

indeed a strange world.

"You're in a hurry to return to America," the Hindu said flashing his great eyes first upon the boy then moving his gaze across to Harvey Dodds. His smile seemed to say that he knew everything even better than the American did himself. "You may rest here in comfort and safety, Captain Dodds. There is little need for you to continue your journey to Allahabad!"

"Sri Jumna," said the boy quickly. "I have brought my friend to the ashram. He will stay here as it is his desire. I am the one who wishes to continue on to Allahabad!"

Jumnaji bowed his head. "God gave man free will to make his decisions. But there is no cause for you to go, young master. We can take care of everything here until the Master returns.

"He left no instructions as what his wishes might be. Nothing was said except that you were coming and the hour of your arrival. The Wheel of Heaven leaves all to God. But my desire is that you enjoy the hospitality of the ashram to await the Guru's joyous return. Time will pass like eternity as it usually does while he is away, but you are safe here and well cared for."

Dodds smiled thinking of that flimsy gate. "I thank you for your kindness, my Lord. But since Shyama wants to proceed to Allahabad, I agreed with him that it is best to go on to Allahabad. There is somewhat of an urgency within me to be directly under the Master's protection."

"As you wish, Captain Dodds," Jumnaji

closed his eyes to a narrow slit and gazed dreamily into the dancing fire. "But you must understand that the protection of Swarachakraji is everywhere. It is omnipresent, within and without. He is the essence of life."

"I understand." Dodds replied smiling as though he understood while Shyama touched his heart with one hand when the words were spoken, in adoration for his Master. "We will leave on the next train for Allahabad."

"It is the will of God that you go," said the brown man clapping his hands for a disciple. "I will arrange for you to have food and shelter while you are here."

CHAPTER 3

R. J. Whitfield flew to Allahabad with Lucia and Murray Price to inspect the site for a Gatewood plant. He left Lucia at the hotel and went out to the location where Whitfield and his superintendent spent most of the day and returned in the late afternoon.

A surging crowd pushed through the streets singing and dancing, but Whitfield took it in a superior, tolerant, amused manner, although he didn't like it for it caused a feeling of insignificance to rise in him. This feeling had always been with him, since childhood, as a driving urge to outshine his fellow man in everything.

Whitfield was a man who knew the psychology of the individual. He was aware that the power of leadership depended on his own talents and presence. His whole theory was that once you felt and knew that presence within, you have most of the inner powers with which to work; more life, energy, power, talent, intelligence and everything. Basically it was this: when you become conscious of the power in the mind, your talents and powers produce more in any given field of activity.

He entered the hotel suite and called for Lucia. "She must have gone out," he said to Price who followed him in. "Wish she hadn't done it in that mob of natives out in the streets. Hey, what's this?"

He picked up an envelope from the telephone table and ripped it open. His face went white and a savage oath burst from his lips. "She's gone!" he exploded. "Violated my orders. Damn that woman!"

"What's the trouble, Chief?"

"Lucia's run off to Kumur to find out if that rumor on that Harvey Dodds is true!"

The other man looked sharply. "Maybe it ain't a rumor!"

Whitfield grabbed up the telephone and put in a call for the American Consul at Allahabad. When he finished talking with the Consul, asking that Lucia be contacted and sent back, he turned back to his plant superintendent and yelled for a drink.

Murray Price mixed him one then asked. "What's wrong with you and this American Dodds? You should be happy to help that poor guy; instead you're acting as though he's your worst enemy!"

"He deserves to rot in a dirty, Red prison. His old man gave my wife the wrong prescription right after Lucia's birth and killed her. I've got proof.

"We were living in my hometown, Four Rivers. My wife was ill for days after Lucia's birth. We had no hospital, and still don't for that matter. I called Doc Dodds, who was drunk, and he gave my wife a prescription that was wrong. She died instantly. Everybody knew what happened but me. The doctors, druggists and all connected in the case swore in court that the prescription was right, but I knew better for the clerk at the drugstore who mixed it said it was completely wrong. Old Dodds buried his mistake.

"I fought it through the court but the medical society backed him, and I lost. You see why I hate Harvey Dodds and would do anything to get even with his family!"

Price grinned. "I will give you a hand, Chief. Dodds is in India! He's at Kumur!"

"What?" Whitfield shouted. "You're lying."

"Wait a minute, Chief! Dodds entered the country a few days ago with a tribe of Nomads who escaped the Reds and stopped at Srinagar, in Kashmir. Lal Ghosh, Mayor of Srinagar, sent his son to that Indian Ashram in Kumur, where he would have protection. It belongs to a Holy Man who is all powerful and not even the Reds would dare touch anyone near him.

"Ghosh's son took the American to Kumur but that wasn't the real purpose. He took that manuscript I spoke to you about, for safe keeping until it can be smuggled out of the country. They plan for Dodds to take it to America!"

"What about this manuscript?" Whitfield demanded.

"I learned about it through a Commie who works for us. It's a collections of poems written by a great ECKANKAR Saint, Fubbi Quantz, reputed to be worth a million dollars to the New York Museum of Arts!"

"How are you going to get your hands on it?"

Price said gleefully. "I've already made arrangements. I bribed one of the Red gang to kidnap Ghosh's daughter. She's in a Red stronghold in the hills. The leader is dancing with joy for he thinks that through Ghosh they will get their hands on Dodds and return him to China!"

"You got something on your mind, Price?"

"Chief, it's a cinch! We can force Ghosh to bring us that manuscript for the girl and get the American too. You get your revenge and a million bucks which we can split!"

Whitfield's fist made the table jump. "By God!" he cried. "You hit the jackpot this time!"

Lucia left Allahabad on the early morning train regretful that the urgency within her was forcing her into this course of action. She would have felt better to have told her father openly, but knowing his egocentric attitude she did what was felt best. She was determined to get to Kumur and investigate the rumor that Harvey Dodds was there. Also she wanted to meet the great Living Master, Swarachakraji, known to all India, as the Wheel of Heaven.

The express reached Kumur at high noon. Lucia got off in the boiling noon light, found a cab whose driver agreed to take her out to the ashram. The driver showed little curiosity in her, so she was satisfied to get to the gates of the ashram without question.

A young Hindu monk dressed in a brown

robe, looking like what she would believe Saint Francis might have been, greeted her at the gates. After a salutation he very courteously inquired about her mission there.

She hesitated, then said. "I have come for an interview with your great Master. Is he here?"

The monk ignored her question but bowed deeply. "You must enter, Sahiba. I will take you to Jumnaji, who is in charge of the ashram for the Master. He will answer all your questions. Please follow me!"

They found Jumnaji sitting on the verandah of an old house teaching several disciples, in the absence of Swarachakraji. The boy motioned for her to be seated in a chair and wait until the lecture was over.

She listened to what the brown-skinned man was saying: "I do not speak with the view to satisfy curiosity or to please the mind or the imagination, but rather to quench the thirst of any of you who are true, sincere and humble seekers. Mental acrobatics, tortuous, complicated philosophical gymnastics are not required, nor is there any necessity to pore for hours over a page or an abstract in order to ascertain the author's meaning.

"The plain truth is too simple for the seeker after complexity, looking for things you do not understand. The intellect creates its own problems and then makes itself miserable trying to solve them. Truth always expresses itself with the greatest simplicity.

"I am trying to bridge the gap between

any studies you may have had, and ECKANKAR, the Path of the ECK Masters, known to the worlds as the Ancient Science of Soul Travel—that is the meaning of the ECK, the Audible Life Current.

"To practice ECK out of curiosity, in search of new sensations or to gain psychic powers is a mistake which is punished with futility, neurosis or even worse. But to put yourself under the Living Master, the Godman, is to have the feet well planted upon the path to the eternal home. Truth is never a thing that one finds, but it is always awakened within us, by the Guru, and it is essential that it does not oppress us, but rather should it lead us back to the Soul, God, and give us freedom. And this is precisely what is realized through ECKANKAR."

He stopped, dismissed his audience and turned his dark, luminous eyes upon the girl. She felt the impact of his gaze as he drew the Indian boy to his side, then stood up clad in a dark red robe.

He said gently. "What may I do for you, my daughter?"

"I have come to see Swarachakraji, the ECK Master," she replied, wondering if this was a dream. "And to learn for myself if there is an American Air Force officer here, named Captain Harvey Dodds, who recently escaped from the Chinese Reds."

A rippling smile crossed the smooth brown flesh of his face as he gazed at her with unblinking eyes. "Swarachakraji, the Godman, is at Allahabad attending the Kumba

Mela. Your American officer went there, seeking him!"

"Oh," she cried in disappointment.

"It is all right, my lady. He will return soon!" The Indian assured her.

"Then the story is true. He is alive?"

Jumnaji bowed his head. "He has escaped the scourge of mankind, but is not yet out of danger. Of course he will be glad to see you. Will you wait here for his return, or do you wish to go back to your father in Allahabad?"

She stared at him with sudden realization of what the Indian said. He knew about her position with her father in Allahabad? How did he know? This was strange. She could not understand it.

She looked again into those deep, jet black eyes only to find a profound depth of mystery. Finally she said. "I will stay here, if you do not mind."

Jumnaji smiled softly. "Yes, it is best. There is no danger to the American as long as he is with the Godman!"

He clapped his hands and the Hindu boy came out of the shade of a nearby tree. Jumnaji said, "Take the lady to Umba. She will take care of her needs until the Master returns!"

The boy picked up her suitcase and walked through the soft gardens, under gentle waving palms until they came to a row of small houses, made of boards and shingles.

Umba was a tiny Hindu girl with big soft eyes and a bright smile. She greeted Lucia with a shy manner and salutation, took her bag without reservation setting it inside the screen door.

After a bath of warm water Lucia lay down on a bed whose mattress was made of straw, in a small cell-like room, wondering what her Park Avenue friends would say if they saw her now. Strange thoughts started creeping through her mind. What would be her reaction to meeting Harvey Dodds in this strange place? Would that old hatred for him, her father always taught her to have against the Dodds, creep back when they met? Why was she doing this?

Captain Harvey Dodds and his young companion got off the train at Allahabad in the torrid mid-afternoon heat. The railroad station was filled with pilgrims. They were so thick that neither of them could hardly walk between the pilgrims.

The city of Allahabad was teeming with people. Some three million white-robed pilgrims packed the streets so tightly that it was torture to push through the crowd. Dodds thought he would drop any moment. Some pilgrims were begging, others seeking a Guru, a teacher, and merchants hawking their wares to the gullible public.

Dodds felt as though he would not be able

to take another step. The swirling mass of people smothered him until it seemed as if his breath would not come. Choking with dust he held the boy. "Won't we ever find the Master?" he gasped.

"We will find him quickly," said the boy moving off between the stores into a lesser crowded area so they could walk freer.

Still in the open fields were another million swarming about. In the distance was the broad, ancient Ganges, the Holy River of the Hindus where countless bathers dipped for the remission of their sins; many were engaged in the solemn rituals of worship before tiny altars; others making devotional offerings, and there was a quaint religious parade of naked Sadhus passing, waving scepters of gold, and silver flags and streamers of velvet, which attracted and held Dodds' attention.

They turned into a long street and walked carefully through the heavy crowd to the corner of an alley where Shyama stood to survey the swirling mass.

Dodds' gaze followed the boy who turned and looked up the alley. Standing motionless at the corner of the far end was a tall, Godlike man gazing at them with a piercing glance. He was instantly familiar to Dodds whose hungry stare took him in a full glance.

The man was fully six feet, six inches tall, broad and husky. His head was bare. His face was bearded and high cheeked. He was dressed in a knee-length blue robe, belted at the waist.

Shyama danced with joy. "Master!" he shouted racing forward to sieze the man. The Master enfolded the boy murmuring his name over in a vibrant voice.

Shyama released him and turned. "This is my friend, Captain Dodds," he said proudly.

A strong brown hand reached out and clasped Dodds in a firm grip sending strong electrical currents into his body. Any nervousness he had was gone in the instant their eyes met. He suddenly felt as though he was looking into the depths of the universe, that he had a conscious awareness of the cosmos, of the life and order of the universe.

"You are welcome!" said a deep, melodious voice.

In that moment Dodds felt all the peace and happiness in his heart flowing from the subtle, gentle touch of the man's hand.

Joy was in the Master's voice as he laughed. "I am overjoyed that you are here. Come let's go to my place where you can eat and rest!"

They followed the tall man to a stone house with a balcony overlooking the Ganges, in the Ram Napal section of the city. This was where Swarachakraji had his Allahabad headquarters. Inside he summoned some of his disciples.

"My friends have come," he said to the disciples. "They are tired and hungry. Feed them and show them a place to rest!"

He turned to Shyama and Dodds. "I will

leave you now to retire to my work with God. This is your home. Captain Dodds, you must rest for the next twelve hours in bed. When you awake tomorrow you will be completely refreshed. Do not take any more of the drugs."

He looked down at the boy. "We will talk later about the precious scroll you are carrying."

The long colors of the morning sky were streaking the eastern horizon as Harvey Dodds crawled out of the little pallet in the large, airy room of the hermitage and shook Shyama out of a deep sleep.

The boy sat up yawning. "I was practically in paradise, my elder brother. You were there with me, but most of all was my beautiful sister. I thought that she was in love with you and you two were to be married!"

"That was a dream, Sammy." Harvey Dodds remarked looking about for soap and water. He found a pan nearby on a shelf with towels and a pitcher of warm water somebody had just left. Beside it was a razor and brush. Smiling he picked them up and felt his chin, thinking of the genuine hospitality these Hindus gave their guests.

Suddenly he became conscious that the

fatigue had left his body. No longer was he nauseated, ill and sick to his stomach. His hand went around his body and he looked into the mirror at his countenance. Yes, it was still himself. Thin, ragged and wearing that air of death upon his brow. But for the first time in two years he felt rested.

"Dreams often come true," Shyama said. "And I caught a love-light in her eyes when she looked at you."

"You're teasing, Sammy," Dodds laughed.

"In our world Souls often meet long before the bodies are acquainted with one another. So let my words fall on your ears."

Smiling Dodds finished shaving and they went into the great hall where the Master met them with a gentle, benign smile. Dodds wondered if the Master thought of anything else but happiness. His great shining eyes saw through all things. They ate in a kitchen where dozens of hungry pilgrims were being fed.

After breakfast they followed the Master and a company of chelas along a path through throngs of worshipers observing the early morning rituals. They came to a great field, which was a natural bowl, ringed by hills. A small wooden platform was in the center of the field where a group of men were sitting. Shyama pointed them out individually as some of the greatest Holy Men in India.

"Swarachakraji is going to speak to them," he said.

"To whom?" Dodds asked sitting down

with the chelas as the Master walked toward the group on the platform.

"Those people," Shyama pointed.

Dodds looked at the hills and saw for the first time the thousands of people who had appeared with the arrival of the Master. The hills were black with people. He had never seen so many and it gave him a feeling of being smothered. A quick panic flashed over him and he coughed hard. Afterwhile it subsided leaving him weak.

"Why are they here?" he asked.

"For Darshan. This is a blessing, or a spiritual benediction which is given to whoever sees the blessed object, the Godman. The *Shariyat-Ki-Sugmad says that bathing in sacred rivers or visiting temples with idols of clay and stone may purify you after a long time, but the saints purify you at sight. These people come to have Darshan by looking at the holy countenance of the ECK Master, who is the greatest spiritual Master in all the world. We call him, the Godman!"

Swarachakraji mounted the platform. Dodds thought that it was the way Jesus looked the day he stood before the people on the mountainside. A nebulous light developed around the Master as he opened his lips and started speaking in Hindustani.

The silence was complete. Hardly a blade of grass moved in the breeze as the voice of the Master swung across the valley and hills rippling as a river. Harvey Dodds didn't

* The Holy Scriptures of those who follow ECKANKAR, Ancient Science of Soul Travel.

know what the man was saying but peace stole into his heart and for the first time he found calm and happiness. With bowed head he listened and apparently dozed off for when he opened his eyes there stood the Master with a lovely smile on his gentle face.

"You have rested, Captain Dodds," he said softly. "That is good. Soon you will feel well again and be able to take the trip back to America."

Dodds got up apologizing for sleeping, but the Master shrugged it off and turned to Shyama to tell him to take the American back to the hermitage for the sun was getting too hot for Dodds.

The two walked for a long time in silence and for some reason hardly any of the thousands of pilgrims were seen. Finally they turned and started along a path by the great river, around a curve in the path Shyama stopped so abruptly that Dodds almost fell over him. In front of them was a dark copper-skinned man who seemed to be the very essence of God.

His dark eyes were large and luminous with deep wisdom. He wore a white tunic and robe, and his face was covered partly by a flowing beard. Striking power flowed from him

Shyama fell to the ground in obeisance to this strange person. Sensing the mysterious power that flowed from this kingly man, Dodds bowed deeply.

The being spoke in a melodious voice as Dodds had never heard before. "It is well that we meet, my friends of God. Stand up for you need not bow to me."

His dark eyes narrowed as if to keep the great shining light from blinding them. It seemed to penetrate directly into Harvey Dodds' soul. It was a light so great that it was like a burning fire. And with it came a strange sound of bagpipes.

"I am Viswapati—Lord of the World. You have my blessings for a great future lies before you to serve God. It is ITS will that you do.

"Have no fear while you are with us, O one from the foreign lands. You are in no danger. You will become one of the followers of ECKANKAR in time to reach perfection with God. You will become a messenger to America for the advent of the ECKANKAR teachings."

With a single glimpse of his magnetic eyes, the man electrified Dodds which seemed to bring out a sense of expanded consciousness. As suddenly as he appeared, the man was gone.

They stumbled back to the hermitage where Swarachakraji was awaiting them. After eating he listened attentively while Shyama excitedly told of their meeting with the Holy Man on the river path.

Swarachakraji said gently, "You were fortunate, my friends. That was Viswapati, Lord of the World. You have witnessed him in the flesh—a glorious privilege which has been visited upon so few of us!"

The boy swooned with delight and Dodds pinched himself to see if this was not a dream. Suddenly Shyama sat up. "Master will you give my brother the initiation?"

The Master laughed. "This is for our guest to decide when he becomes better acquainted with our philosophy. Now come, we must prepare to leave tonight on the train for Kumur. There isn't much time left!"

They got on the train late that night and rode through the night while Shyama tried to explain the text of the speech that the Master had delivered that morning.

After awhile the great Master looked up from his seat, cross-legged on the floor. "Captain Dodds, you must return to America as soon as possible. Duty calls you there to finish your work in medicine. There is yet a debt to be paid someone in the city of your birth, which can only be done by going back. There is extreme danger for your life as long as you stay in India. When you pay this debt, which was created by your father, you will return to me to learn what is the next step in your life's journey to God. Regard my words seriously!"

Lucia passed her days in quiet happiness awaiting the return of the Living Master and his devotees. There was a magical tranquility about this wonderful place which gave her for the first time in her life a peace, which seemed to issue out of the very air around her.

She did a great deal of thinking during

this period, especially about her past life and her father's relationship with her. She wondered if this life was meant for herself to live and be near the great Soul, Swarachakraji and those who dwell in his ever spreading light.

A few days later she was sitting on the verandah enjoying date nuts and sweets with Jumnaji and the disciples when a shout arose from the gates. She stood up quickly. Looking out she saw a group of travelers, in white-cowled robes, entering the Ashram grounds.

"The Master!" shouted one of the chelas springing to his feet and rushing toward the tall one with a shining Godlike countenance, who was in the lead of the little party.

Instantly the yard was filled with people bowing to this tall, distinguished, bearded man. Others tried to kiss his hand but he withdrew it, smiled benignly and walked on to the porch where he greeted Jumnaji and the disciples. He seemed to electrify the air.

Lucia watched with a pounding heart. It was as though she was a pair of eyes without a body recording an event. Perhaps a motion picture camera that caught an important event for the newsreels, but the newsreel was her brain and it would play back this scene in her life many times.

She was aware of this yet there was not an emotion in her body, not a sensation nor feeling. Strange, wasn't it? She was only aware of space, and time and of God. Why, this was God? Could she be sure of that thought!

She captured it and tucked it away neatly in one corner of her mind like filing a letter. When time permitted she would take it out and examine it again.

The tall man with the beautiful countenance slowly turned and let his luminous eyes fall upon her. In that brief moment she felt a terrible tearing in her heart. The flood gates of her emotions broke loose like water overflowing a dam. Then suddenly she realized that tears were coursing down her cheeks.

He took her hands in his. His eyes were soft, gentle, and penetrating with a depth of wisdom which she could not understand. His touch was electrifying and left a peacefulness within her heart.

"Welcome to this Ashram, my daughter," his voice was the gentle wind in the trees, the rushing water over stones. "You have been a long time coming home. But now you are here and we will enjoy your stay with us."

She looked at him with numbness, embarrassed by her tears, not knowing what was wrong with herself. He turned and pulled a man out of the crowd who looked as though he had come from the grave. "This is the man for whom you have long searched. Captain Dodds. We will leave you two alone to talk over private matters.

"Come Shyama and we will go to my hut and see if there is any food. Afterwards we will find work if there is any to be done. Surely, there must be for I know that everybody has been sleeping since I've been away."

His laughter was a string of beads rolling into space.

Lucia looked into the deep, tired eyes of the gaunt man standing before her and a terrible shock ran through her. She shook like a tree limb in a heavy gale. That face was of a man who had seen too much of life. She would have never recognized Harvey Dodds anywhere else.

She whispered. "Harvey, is that you?"

"Lucia Whitfield?" his voice echoed.

"Yes, it is I."

They stood there staring at one another across the space for what seemed to be eternity. Pity for this man rolled through her heart in a terrible storm of agony.

Finally he said, "What are you doing here? Six thousand miles from New York?"

"I am here with father. He is on a business trip. I got word that you were here and needed help, so I came."

"Thank God," his voice almost broke. "Then the American Ambassador knows where I am?"

"Not yet, Harvey. I came here on a wild chance. In fact I even had to slip away from R.J., at Allahabad where he was on a business trip, to get here. He is going to be really angry about it. Tonight I'll send him a wire and one to the American Ambassador to tell them where you . . ."

Suddenly she broke off and stared wildly at the strong figure of a man striding across the open space of the yard. That was the same man in the hotel lobby who told about Harvey? No! Her eyes were failing her. It couldn't be. She wiped them with her hands and looked again.

"What is it?" Dodds asked quickly.

"That man. There! Who is he? I want to speak to him!" she cried pointing.

Harvey Dodds whirled and caught sight of a strong looking man in a maroon robe disappearing behind a building. He saw him make a movement then check himself.

"I don't know, Lucia," he said shrugging his shoulders. "Why I guess it's just another disciple around here. The woods are full of them in India. Did he disturb you?"

She wiped her eyes carefully with a handkerchief. "No, Harvey. I guess that I'm just worked up over seeing you. It doesn't matter now that you are back from the dead."

Somebody appeared on the far side of the yard. Looking up, she saw a policeman and the Master approaching. A few feet away the Guru stopped. "My daughter," he said. "This officer of the law has come to take you back to your father in Allahabad. You must go with him."

She started to speak but he stopped her with a raised hand. "It is best that you go. You will come back to me again at the time which will be of your own free nature when there is nobody to protest it.

"Do not worry about Captain Dodds for we have already informed the proper American authorities where he is and soon he will be in that wonderful country of America. There you will meet again. But meanwhile there is much to be done before you can return to the Ashram. Your father will pay his debt to Karma and you will suffer much but will have a greater understanding of life!"

The Hindu boy came up beside Swarachakraji his eyes shining with a wonderful light. The Master put his arm around the boy's shoulders. Smiling gently he pulled him closely and let his keen glance slide from the girl across to Harvey Dodds.

"Captain Dodds," his voice was grave and deep. "You must take Shyama with you to America. The manuscript which he is carrying is exceedingly important to the world. His life is in danger as long as he has it in his possession. There are many in India who would murder him without thought for his part in the transfer of the scrolls to Kumur.

"Keep him in America until it is safe for his return. I will furnish the money for his transportation and make arrangements with his parents to care for his expenses while living with you. Take care of him though he were your own son!"

CHAPTER 4

Captain Harvey Dodds came home to Four Rivers. After months of suffering and a flight half-way across the world he reached the little town where his life had been spent, hoping this would be his haven of peace.

He stood by the window of the stairwell, in his home, looking at the river. The late afternoon light was a shimmering glow on the blue Mississippi flowing past the empty levee and joining the muddy Ohio at the city's waterfront. This was the eternal river, so different from the Holy Ganges, never changing in its nature and austere beauty. It moved unhurriedly and without pause, year after year, past green banks filled with fairy willows.

An old crane fished lazily on the point of the Island, and from the distance came a ring of calking mallets at the river docks. They were the oldest riverboat docks in the nation. There General Ulysses S. Grant built the first river gunboat for a great victory at Fort Henry and Donaldson.

The river wind swept the street lifting the aftermath of a gala parade for his homecoming. Overhead banners swayed and sagged as though they like himself wanted to rest. The racking cough shook him and he thought of his old friend Tien Batir. Would he still be alive? And could Shyama fit himself into this narrow existence of life after the broad concepts of cosmic feeling which had been found at the ECKANKAR Ashram in Kumur?

Except for his cough the Army medical officers had declared him in good health. He dared not tell them that it was the Living Master, Swarachakraji, who had completely healed him by a mere touch of his hand.

The house had belonged to his family for generations, and Aunt Carrie Dodds, a spinster, his only living relative and a great philanthropist, had taken charge of Harvey Dodds and his young companion from the time they touched the soil of America.

The old house was set upon a broad span of land overlooking the Mississippi. The double story structure was built in 1811, a year after the great earthquake shook the region. It had been the headquarters for General Andrew Jackson when he purchased the territory between the rivers from the Chickasaw Indians.

Sitting at the table after the evening meal Aunt Carrie Dodds said disgustedly, "Men are like children. It takes a woman to get them on the right path. Harvey, you'll get two days in bed and then start your practice. Work will cure you quicker than anything else. I've kept your offices and your medical equipment. Plenty of patients need you in town!"

He saw her glance across at Shyama. She had put her influence over both men and guided them into a narrow course which was dissatisfying and repelling. Her firm belief was that the boy was a heathen sent to her doorstep to be rescued and saved for God.

She was tall, sparse with rugged features and brooked no opposition to her will. Religion was her forte and anyone who was not a member of her church stood, in her fixed opinion, in terrible danger of losing his Soul to eternal damnation and hell's fire.

"What about Sammy?" he asked reluctantly.

"Put him to work earning his board and keep. He can tend the house, sweep, carry out the garbage and do general work. I'll fix up a room in the garage for him. That's the only place for people with a dark skin!"

Harvey Dodds said angrily, "He will be a guest in this house as long as he is here. Or I will move out and take him with me. What do you want to do, Sammy?"

"Go to school and learn to be a doctor like yourself," the boy said defiantly. "My father will take care of the expenses after I sell the manuscript."

"That settles it," Dodds said, laying his napkin aside. "I will take care of you. It will cost you nothing, Auntie, except to see that he is well cared for and that you are courteous to him."

She snapped. "What is that dirty old paper he keeps with him all the time? Get rid of it or I'll take it away from him and do it myself!"

"No." Dodds said firmly. "That is an extremely important document and worth a great deal of money. I have to go to New York soon and see about selling it. We underwent great danger to bring it out of India and might get into further trouble if you talk about it in public!"

He got up and went outside in the rich twilight. Turning he looked at the old white shingled house that seemed to hang against the green leaves of great oaks that grew over the roof. The vast sky was wider, higher with a richer blue than he had thought possible.

He did not yet feel right about this old house nor the town. There was so little warmth in it. The old, degenerated and odd currents of feeling which swept through the invisible atmosphere seemed to touch him negatively and bring out that side of himself. He did not like this. Inwardly, he flinched against it. The struggle within his Soul was heightening.

Six thousand miles away in Srinagar, Lal Ghosh sat in his library, his head drooping despondently. He held a crude written letter in his hand which had been delivered an hour before. It was the first information about his daughter since her disappearance.

He and his wife had been driven almost to the verge of broken health from their grief. The kidnappers had played the game wisely. They had not revealed anything about Amiya and timed the emotional value of her unexpected absence upon Ghosh's nerves. Then came this message demanding the ancient scroll of Fubbi Quantz's poems to be brought to a certain place in the Himalayas by Captain Dodds.

The plot was thinly disguised but effective. They were going to succeed in getting the manuscript and Dodds again with one hook. Ghosh felt a keen sense of awful fear dragging him down into the depths of despair. He seldom recognized defeat but this time he had met with failure because his enemies had the most precious thing of his life in their hands.

Ghosh was normally supplied with abundant energy, powerful constitution, and a considerable amount of personal courage and usually won the goal he strove for. But this time he was cast into a frozen mold of fear for his daughter's safety and nothing would stand in his way of getting her back.

He left the library and went to the bedroom where his wife was already retired. He took her hands and looked deeply into her eyes. She was a distinctly feminine woman, small, bright-eyed and only too happy to serve him without chafing the intellectual egotism in him. He was always too sure of himself and prone to dominate situations which alienated the very persons most useful to him, but she knew him well and kept in the background only to serve him and his cause.

He told her about the letter and she said, "What will you do, my husband?"

"I will send a telegram to the Master to hold the American until I arrive." He replied gruffly, hoping that none of the deep agony in his heart would make him tremble before her. "Then I will take the first plane for Kumur and bring him and my son here. The American will not be told what my plan is so that his capture by the Reds will be easy and won't make trouble for us!"

Late that afternoon Lal Ghosh left for Kumur by plane and arrived there within a few hours. He went straight to the Ashram to seek out Swarachakraji.

The Ashram grounds were familiar to him. Beyond were the misty blue hills and that awful gulch on the other side of the grounds which dropped for hundreds of feet into the valley. Beyond that was the river singing past the Ashram wall, making its way across the countryside toward the Holy Ganges.

The Master met him at the door of his hut, tall, grave and smiling his welcome. He returned Ghosh's salutation and invited him to enter. The Mayor entered the little hut and seated himself upon the straw mat usually reserved for visitors. He sat in silence awaiting the Master to speak, listening to the wind make little whistling sounds around the corner of the hut.

Finally the Master spoke in his deep voice which could hardly be distinguished from the wind. "You've come to speak about Amiya. You are deeply grieved over her disappearance!"

"Of course, Master!" Lal Ghosh cried

loudly. "I need your help, sire! I want my daughter back at once. The note says she will be returned safely if the American Air Officer will bring the scroll to them on Friday. Where is my son and Captain Dodds?"

"Be calm, sir!" Swarachakraji's eyes glistened brightly in the half-light of the hut. "Be not hasty in your actions. Trust in God!"

"Where are they?" Ghosh demanded. "Didn't you receive my telegram?"

"Do not question my instructions but follow them out completely. That is all, my son. Farewell and be true to your own self. That is all that I ask of you."

Harvey Dodds could not forget the great Living ECK Master. The image of the gentle, loving Soul was constantly in his inner vision. He stared continually at the vision no matter what passed before his exterior gaze. It gave him an intense look which appeared to be always smiling. His countenance was thin, pale and high-boned, with gray eyes set far back in their sockets. But that look which he had brought home with him from the war puzzled his friends.

He worked daily at his office without complaint, but his stare annoyed some and frightened others. They never understood that it was the deeper self looking through his eyes broodingly upon a world in which only his body lived.

Soul was all that was left of Harvey Dodds. The flame within him had burnt away everything else like dross. Nothing else important remained in him but the spirit which stood out strongly even after the sickness of his body was gone. Now it was a sickness of the spirit.

He knew that Shyama was bothered with the same problem of the self for the boy was barred from returning to his home in India. Both had to stay in Four Rivers to fulfill a destiny which God had set for them. Even the Godman had told them that.

He was alone this day in his office in the highest building of the city. He could look out the window at the movement of boats along the waterfront, a scene he never forgot even in the dark, dank prison in China. The misty hills beyond the shining waters of the river mirrored the other shores. Flat, golden sandbars poked long fingers into the river giving him a nostalgic memory of boyhood days, canoeing and swimming along those shores.

A friend, Jesse Adams, called and said a party was to be given Harvey that evening at the Country Club. Reluctantly Harvey agreed and at eight-thirty that night, with Shyama, he pushed into the club where a band was playing melodic waltzes and liquor flowed freely.

Discord struck him instantly. There was something within him unprepared for this.

His guard had dropped so completely that he no longer knew how to protect himself. His interval with Swarachakraji had left him without defense against any coarse vibrations of life.

But he put on a cheerful face and greeted all as though he liked this. Shortly afterward he paired off with a slender girl named Julie Vanners, daughter of a minister in Four Rivers, where his aunt attended church.

Julie was pretty, had a good figure, was an excellent dancer and had good intelligence which made for conversation with most men. Harvey liked her quick sympathy and her sensitivity on subtle points.

"I had a note from Lucia the other day," she said while dancing. "She's back in New York. Apparently there has been trouble between her and R. J."

"Oh?" he lifted his eyebrows in question.

"I'm not sure about the trouble between them. She hinted something about leaving him for good. They have separated and she's living in her own apartment. Said she might be home soon. Asked about you."

"I'll always be grateful to Lucia for finding me in India," he said as the music stopped and they walked toward the punchbowl. "Hers was the first familiar face I had seen in two years."

"Harvey," she said suddenly. "You're not happy here are you? What was it you found in India that makes you so dissatisfied with Four Rivers? What gives you that strange look in your eyes?"

He turned and pushed her outside onto

the porch where the stars blinked overhead like a million jewels and the light breeze rustled through the oak leaves. A slow fire started burning in his heart.

He said," I didn't know it was so apparent, or perhaps you are only guessing something is wrong with me. Nobody else has said that to me. They seem to think, or at least make me think, it's normal living here with my aunt. I found something in India. Yes, I found myself but left it there and would like to go back for it."

"A woman?" she whispered.

He felt strange talking about this. "It was a man. Now I can't go back. This is the world where I belong. Forgive me, Julie, but let's go in again, and then I must leave. This party doesn't meet with the new ideals I've developed."

"Who is that boy with you. And why is he with you constantly?"

Dodds laughed. "Maybe my twin Soul. I don't know. He saved my life out there in India and I, by chance, saved his, and he has sworn to stay with me until the debt is evened up. That is his philosophy and I must say I like having him around."

"Doesn't he cost you money?" she asked wide-eyed.

"His father is wealthy and helps with the expenses. He's like having my own son around."

She caught his hands and kissed him. It was like the sweetness of the morning dew. He said, "If I were the man I should be, Julie, I'd ask you to marry me and settle down to a life of marital bliss."

She said. "It makes little difference, Harvey. Just to be near you makes me happy."

"No. You marry Jesse Adams," he said. "He's crazy about you and will give you more happiness than I. I belong to someone else and can never be shared with any one person."

"Please call me sometime, Harvey. Please."

He promised and walked into the ballroom to motion for Shyama to leave. They went to the car and got into it. Driving toward the city he knew that this was the moment for him to take a long walk along the river front to contemplate on Swarachakraji.

He turned to the boy. "Sammy, there is a letter on my desk from the Chicago Museum. They want to see the manuscript. I will make an appointment with them for the first of next week and we can take it to them. All must be done in strict secrecy for there are many in this country who would be most happy to steal it."

"I don't feel good about this either, Harvey," said the boy. "There are some strange people following me of late. I don't understand. Somebody has been watching the house lately, from about midnight on to morning. I have seen them."

Harvey Dodds gave a start. Could it be possible that somebody had followed them all the way from India? Strange as it was, they had never heard anything from Bhola Lal Ghosh, yet he and Shyama both had written him several times.

He must not let the boy see that this news disturbed him. "Let's forget about it. It is nothing. But Sammy can you tell me about God? Now I want to know more than anything else in the world. What is the most important thing to know about God?"

"Love," said the boy, turning his brilliant eyes upon Dodds. "Love is the greatest aspect of God. Find love and you find God."

"But how does one go about seeking love?" he asked straining at the thought in his mind, trying to frame the question right and make it seem as if he weren't trying to side track Sammy from the danger in which he might be.

"Through ECKANKAR," Shyama said softly. "That is the true path to God. All Masters who have come in the past have taught that the ECK, the sound current is the way to reach God."

Two days later he was in his office when the nurse announced that Julie Vanners was in the reception room. Dodds shook off his dreams of the Master and asked that she be shown in.

Julie Vanners came into the office smiling and gave him a cheerful handshake. But her touch stayed just a little too long and too intimately in front of the nurse. Harvey Dodds pulled his hand away and offered her a chair.

He faced her across the desk thinking she looked disturbed despite her gay manner and charm which seemed to ooze from her. "Tell me what is the latest news from Lucia?" he asked.

"Only one letter since I saw you last. She was on her way to California. Will be there a few months but coming through Four Rivers on her way back to New York. I hope it will be very soon. I'd like very much to see Lucia again."

"So would I," he said. "Is this a professional or social call? I've got a hunch that you're going to tell me about wedding bells with Jesse Adams?"

She shook her head. "I've broken off with him."

"Well," he said awkwardly. "Now what seems to be the problem with you?"

"I don't know, Harvey," she said with seriousness.

He smiled but his thoughts were on the Master. For a moment he stared at the wall, and straight at the vision of Swarachakraji before him. Everytime his patience grew thin or some problem arose that image of the Godman came into his vision. He would have to ask Shyama about it sometime.

"Oh, yes. Thank you for being kind to Sammy. He told me how you're helping him with his English during the evenings."

She gave him a shy glance. "I enjoy it. He's teaching me so many things too."

Instantly he knew that the girl had invited Shyama into her house, to learn about himself, just to be near somebody who was close to him.

"All right, Julie," he said. "Let's start somewhere. You have any aches or pains?"

She twisted her handkerchief. "I've been awfully sick at my stomach lately and feel queer most of the time."

"No cause for alarm," he said gently rejecting the thought in his mind. "I'll have Miss Wolfe take some blood samples, then do a routine check on you. I can call you about it in a couple days."

"You keeping anything from me, Harvey?"

"Why do you say that, Julie?"

"No reason, at all. Just guilt feelings. Guess I'll have to tell you. You're my doctor!"

He laughed gently. "Don't shoo up the chickens before they've hatched, Julie. You might be overwrought from your trouble with Jesse Adams."

Amiya Ghosh followed the man out of the darkness of the hut into the morning sunlight. For a few minutes she stood blinking to adjust her vision to the day, then saw Nath Dwark sitting on a log in the tree shade. She stiffened, pulled herself erect to hold her body in irons while the storm raged within her.

The air was chilly. She pulled the robe

around her shoulders, shivering a little. There was a strange beauty in the foothills. Breathless in more sense than one, she stood praying for strength and gazing until the distant, snow-capped mountains, so unearthly and yet of the stuff of the earth, seemed to pass into her, bracing and stiffening her in every faculty and fibre for the task to face Nath Dwark.

The big, dark face of the man was relaxed, but grim in its image against the pattern of her mind. He silently beckoned her to come closer. The sun-light splashed through the tree leaves behind him, leaving his features obscured in the shadows.

"Bring her a stool!" his voice was rough in its order to one of the ragged riflemen standing behind him, but she stopped the man with a shake of her head.

"I'll stand to listen to what you have to say." Her voice was low but sharp and cutting to the point. She could see the reaction in his eyes.

She was a person who would cling tenaciously to her decision and make a valiant struggle toward any goal which she set for herself. She had chosen to fight for her freedom with every womanly wile instead of yielding to any demands that Dwark or the American Murray Price had made for her to regain her liberty.

"Are you comfortable?" he asked in an almost gentle voice. After she nodded, he added, "I will do anything to relieve your suffering Amiya Ghosh. You are very beautiful and should I have not been put in the position as these circumstances demand, it might have been my privilege to someday ask for your hand in marriage."

The words brought a sudden shock. A stillness came over her as she stood immobile and rigid with her long, slim fingers clasped tightly. She saw with astonishing clarity the depths of this man's heart, the breaking away of the hard crust which surrounded it. The vision of the endless distances of all the future and the suffering he had in the past and would undergo, passed in her mind. There were the tomorrows which he would have to confront and master, if he would come to God.

She stared at him, dark-eyed, with an arid emptiness of feeling that was objective in its meaning, but now seeping back into some hidden corner of her brain to be kept for future purpose. This man understood a woman's hunger for love, and her need for a man's protection from the unknown qualities of life. His words just proved that. He had embraced her inwardly, thinking he could give her comfort, by his words, which were not lies, but truth spoken from the innermost depths of his heart. Yet this was his fate, for he was caught up in a web of karma of his own making. Within his heart was a profound adoration for her yet he could not express it, nor could she take advantage of his feelings. And she knew that he was wise in his understanding of herself.

"What is it that you wish of me, Nath Dwark?" she asked in a voice that was well under control but trembled inwardly at this newly discovered knowledge.

"I've a message from your father. He says the American Officer and your brother are already in America. That leaves me empty-handed and unable to account to my comrades."

"I don't understand. Why did my brother go to America?" she asked in confusion.

"Apparently he was sent by Swarachakra-ji, the ECK Master who believed he would be safe there but I understand that Whitfield, the capitalist, will have his men murder your brother for that scroll."

She rubbed her hands together tightly. "May I go home now?" she murmured.

Dwark's head shook his answer. "No, Amiya. You are Mr. Price's prisoner, not mine. But I will do whatever possible for your comfort. Meanwhile if you wish to send a message to your family I'll see that it is delivered. Tomorrow I'll bring a woman to help you with cooking."

"I'll send the message," she said sadly turning into the cave knowing the torment burning in her eyes. It would consume her if one ounce of her faith in God was dropped. She would live in terror and knowledge that her family also suffered.

Rosha brought her pen and ink and she wrote the message, then laid down upon the blankets. The events of time marched through her consciousness. She realized that she was doomed regardless.

She knew this for a certainty. She accepted it as a part of her karma. She even smiled a little to think how clearly it could become when faced with it and able to watch things march by while reviewing them, waiting patiently for meaning and end to show itself. But she knew the end—that Nath Dwark possessed great love for her. This was love without volition, almost without consciousness. It came willingly and unbidden to reveal the sum of all her yesterdays and the horizon of her future.

It resolved itself in her mind to know that somewhere in her heart was a feeling that kept growing for this wild adventurer—the scourge of Kashmir.

Shyama came home from school on Friday afternoon in a mixed mood. He was worried over his father's letter, received several days before, and though it sounded cheerful he detected it wasn't right. And there was that prowler who kept watching his window at night. He knew that somebody was waiting to put their hands on that manuscript. It had to be guarded with his life.

Also, he was feeling good over the fact that tonight he had his first date with an American girl, one of the local college students. Most of the students avoided him because of his dark skin. They whispered behind his back but he pretended not to notice.

Martha Long seemed to disturb him somehow, deep within himself. He wasn't sure of what it might be that she did to him for that feeling came into his heart just by looking at her in class. He wanted to find out. He wanted to touch her white skin, feel her copperish hair in his hands and learn the mystery behind those cool-green mocking eyes.

A letter was at the house for him. Miss Carrie was in the living room sewing when he came in. She gave him a long glance. "You're in a peculiar mood today," she said penetratingly.

He gave a start. She almost read his mind. His principal fault was that of his intensity of feelings and secretiveness. The two factors resulted in an extremely complex and highly tense life. He said nothing and went up to his room where he checked the tiny wall safe behind the Monet painting to see if the manuscript was still there. Satisfied he laid across the bed and opened the letter. The vibrancy of the handwriting come out at him. It was from the Master.

Kumur, Oudha, India
September 29, 1954

My Son:

You have asked a question and the answer must be given. You are inquisitive about the ECK Power. This power is the great force of God, Spirit, an omnipotent force which is prevalent throughout the worlds of Cosmic

— 83 —

Reality. It is the intelligent force that fashions the smallest flower and the greatest planet alike, and controls and directs the countless suns and worlds in their orbits, that underlies and fills all, from the small to the large.

Everything is a manifestation of this great power, which has throughout eternity worked toward the ever-increasing expression of its own ineffable fullness. The word of God is written in the heart of the acorn. And it is also within the Soul of man—that living word which is the ECK Power, the same Word of which St. John wrote. In the fullness of time the acorn is born of the music of the Word, unfolds itself and discloses its strength as the oak tree, and likewise wisdom, love and power are unfolded in man.

Law and order is obtained in one growth, just as in the other. You must have spiritual realization now, in this life, for what can be promised you after you leave death. The physical body is the vehicle through which you attain unity with God. The ideal, the goal in embryo, is that which we forever seek. God! One might say, all that a Soul may ever hope to become, is at this moment, at every moment, locked within that Soul's depth. Each Soul contains at any and every stage of its existence the history of its own past and the prophecy of its future.

You can have God-Realization now, this moment, but one must make up his mind to do so. We always dwell in eternity. If I go to Paris or London, I have traveled over distance, but in the eyes of God, I have gone nowhere. Neither do I travel anywhere within the spheres of the first three worlds, in its time, space, energy and matter. We do not go anywhere within these Cosmic worlds. How can we? We are in eternity always. Here, now!

The Light and Sound are your pillars. Keep them to your heart always and you will never be without God.

Swarachakra

The words were still in Shyama's mind as he sat with the girl, Martha Long, on her porch thinking about India and his intimate life in the Kashmir vales.

Suddenly she rolled herself around against him, pushed one arm around his neck and kissed him. The very action startled him but instant delight filled his body. She was like a jasmine blossom which touched too heavily would break of its own fragility. His mind swooned and a great whirling of his senses sent him into an ecstacy of joy. His body and mind hung between the outer and inner spaces of the worlds.

Suddenly something made him pull back sharply. He could have sworn that there stood in the shadows of the vines behind the swing, the strong figure of Rebazar Tarzs as was seen on the road to Punjab. He thought of the manuscript in the wall safe in his room.

Without a word he jumped from the porch and raced down the street calling on the Master. He wanted to go home to India.

A man ran across the street into the dark alley. Shyama did not see him. He ran up the steps into the house, threw open the door, nobody was there. Quickly and silently he ran up to his room and threw on the light switch.

The disheveled state of his room met his stunned gaze. His clothes were scattered over the room and the bed clothing was strewn across the floor. The dresser drawers were pulled out and thrown upside down. The Monet had been torn from the wall and the safe door was gaping like an open mouth.

With a cry of despair he flung himself toward the open safe. The manuscript was gone.

CHAPTER 5

Nath Dwark sat in his swivel chair, in his office at Srinagar, puzzled over the problem of the girl in his hill camp. His stark, proud face was wreathed in a dark frown which drew together three vertical lines etched deeply between his brows.

He looked through the window at the valley of the Kashmir, lying wide and peaceful under the warm autumn sunlight. Beyond, the lofty snows of the Himalayas hung impalpably in a cloudless sky. This was his world but it had gone to pieces because of the girl.

Rosha pushed open the door, closed it behind him and crossed the floor to the desk. Any moment Dwark's temper might tear apart and kill his henchman for making that mistake in kidnapping the girl.

"What is it?" he asked gruffly.

"Chung Ling is here. He wants to see you!"

"Chung Ling!" Dwark exclaimed.

Chung Ling, the dreaded administrator of the Chinese Intelligence Service, was in Kashmir. "So Ling's got here at last. Where is he?" Dwark asked.

"At the hotel. He says come at once!"

Dwark arose from his chair, a giant in his orange pantaloons and embroidered vest. His right hand snaked out and caught Rosha by the shoulder. "Can I trust you?" he demanded.

"Yes, master!" Rosha growled.

"Get a couple of men and post them around the hotel. You stay by the door. If

I need help I'll whistle. Come at once!"

A few minutes later he rapped hard on a hotel door. It was opened by a hard-faced Oriental, but Dwark brushed by him and entered to find a squat, broad man with double chins and pop eyes sitting in a chair.

Ling took a cigar from his mouth and said. "You fool!"

Dwark stood silently awaiting the words that would spew violently from the man. He was fully aware that the doorman was behind him.

"You bungled that job we had for you. The American got away. What are you going to do about it?"

"Nothing!" Dwark laughed softly.

Ling whispered menacingly. "If you weren't needed to get party control of the city government, I'd have you removed!"

Dwark smiled. "What are you going to do?"

"You've got Ghosh's daughter up at your camp. She's my ace in the hole. You go to Ghosh and tell him that the girl will be released provided he signs a statement supporting you as Mayor in the next election!"

"What if I don't do this?" Dwark said swiftly.

A flat laugh cracked Ling's mouth. "You'll do what I tell you or that girl won't live very long."

Dwark lunged at the ugly face but a pair of arms caught him from behind, pinned him back. He stood panting hard staring at the grinning man. "You got her?" He breathed with difficulty.

Ling nodded silently.

"Then I'll carry out your orders." Dwark said quietly shrugging off the gripping arms. "What do you want me to do?"

Ling grinned triumphantly.

Harvey Dodds looked at his appointment calendar on the desk. His countenance was pale and there was deep suffering in his eyes. His mind whirled like crazy from the loss of that manuscript. Shyama was at home, sick, trying to recover from the shock. Dodds could not understand who, in America, would know about the manuscript being in his home.

A telephone call came from Mrs. Walton, president of the Women's Club. She said, "The Women's Club invites you to give a talk before its members and guests, about your experiences in India among the religious sects there!"

He breathed deeply thinking this was not the time to talk about ECKANKAR but he didn't shake Mrs. Walton. He finally said, "All right, when do you want it?"

"Tuesday night in the club auditorium. Thank you, Doctor!"

He hung up the phone thinking that it would be all right to give them a little and receive a few polite handshakes. A good deed done for a few bored people who were living adventure second-handed.

The phone rang again. The Chief of Police talked with Harvey for some length about the robbery and finally asked if Dodds knew anything about an old manuscript from India, reported to be in the city. Dodds denied knowledge, then was asked if he knew a Murray Price. The Chief explained he had a report from New York about such a manuscript and that a man named Price was after it.

That evening Dodds asked Shyama about this. The boy said, "Yes, I know the name. He's a worker for Miss Whitfield's father. He runs the Gatewood plant at New Delhi!"

"Good Lord!" Dodds exclaimed.

Then he dropped the subject and asked what he should talk about at the Women's Club meeting.

"Contemplate like the Master told you and he will come and tell you what to say," Shyama replied.

When Harvey Dodds stepped to the rostrum that Tuesday evening before an audience of prominent men and women of Four Rivers, he was nervous wondering what he was going to say. Then he opened his mouth and to his surprise began his talk. He told about his escape from China with the help of the Kazakhs, the time spent at the ashram with the Master and then ECKANKAR.

"ECKANKAR is the art of going within one's self to make contact with the audible life stream, the sound current, within the body.

"This sound current, or Voice of God, is known to all great religions, but which means the Science of ECKANKAR. It is called the art of Soul Travel.

"Any philosophical system or religion which does not make both the Light and Sound the central portion of its spiritual exercises can never withstand the downward drag of mind and matter. And what is still more important, that without the Light and Sound, the disciple cannot go far toward spiritual liberation.

"The true Living ECK Master teaches that contacting the Inner Light and Sound is essential for spiritual progress. The practice of the ECK exercises in ECKANKAR and a Living ECK Master must go together.

"Swarachakraji, of Allahabad, India, Spiritual Leader of ECKANKAR, the living group who represents ECK here on earth, is the Living Master belonging to the tradition of the ECK Adepts of the Ancient Order of Vairagi, like Rebazar Tarzs. He teaches you to see the Light and listen to the ECK Sound Current.

"The teachings of the adepts lay stress on both inner Light and Sound. The Light is necessary for the traveling Soul to see pitfalls and obstructions enroute, and the Sound is to enable it to follow the source from whence it emanates. These two aspects of the Word need to be contacted within. They exist in the latent form in all human beings. It is a true Master who discovers them for us, gives inner contact and we make progress toward our eternal home.

"We must take the first step and find a Living ECK Master, a genuine Sat-Guru, and be initiated by him. We will not make any real advancement on the path until this is done.

"The Living Master is a Godman: He is God personified or the ECK personified. He is the true competent Master who works for the freedom of the enslaved Souls, leading them beyond out of the Physical, the Astral and the Causal planes of existence.

"The path is a practical one and cannot be learned from books or those versed in books. It can be learned only from a Living ECK Master, who at the time of the initiation imparts detailed instructions on the inner path, explains the practical difficulties and gives the actual inner experience of the Light and Sound Current to all who sit for this initiation. This experience has to be developed by daily meditation—at fixed hours is helpful. Any easy and comfortable posture would do for the purpose. The attention is to be fixed upon a spot between and behind the eyes technically known as the Tisra Til or Third Eye.

"The Master stresses that one should fix one's gaze within with all love. The effort should be effortless. Equal attention must be paid to the Sound Current. Usually the Light appears first and then the Sound and then the radiant form of the ECK Master will appear of itself. When he does appear we must absorb our attention into him.

"The sound is developed through the different planes. Each plane has a distinct Sound of its own, though all of them emanate from the same source—the difference being caused by the varying degrees of density resulting from different proportion of matter and spirit in each plane.

"Once you have learned the spiritual exercises in the right way, Soul is literally withdrawn from the physical temple to progress to the higher planes from whence it came. Once the inner life is realized, the outer one begins to seem unreal and of little consequence."

He paused. "If we knew God, as the whole, meaning that if all of us were capable of having wisdom there would be many things in life that would be understandable. We could have conception of the slightest and greatest things. We would understand the economic struggle of the masses—and those who have control of our destiny by such individual capitalists, like R. J. Whitfield, and others who have control of money and power currents.

"Believe what you will, I have tried to tell you what I have come to know about this way of life as taught by the Living ECK Master, Swarachakraji, whose name means the Wheel of Heaven."

R. J. Whitfield's phone rang. He picked it up and listened as his face turned fiery red. He slammed down the receiver and spoke into the black box on the desk corner asking for a copy of the morning New York Times.

When the girl brought it in, he told her angrily, "Get Carter on the phone, at Four Rivers. Send Able and Jones in here!"

Elsa Spain had the call put through immediately. Whitfield seized the telephone. "Carter, what's this stuff going on down at your plant?" he yelled. "The Times carried an A.P. story on a demonstration against the plant which was created by a talk made by Dr. Dodds!"

Carter's voice was nervous. "Dr. Dodds made a talk the other evening at the Women's Club on India's religions and brought your name in to say you're practicing injustice against mankind by having control of the masses. My wife was there. She didn't like it at all.

"Then some screwballs in the plant got to talking against you and the plant policy. I fired the worst and as a result the whole crew got mad and went out on strike."

Whitfield exploded. "Get them back. We've got that Navy contract which gives us thirty days to produce. One idle week and we lose two million dollars."

"I've hit a snag, Mr. Whitfield. The Union has stepped in and asked for a renegotiation of its contract!"

Whitfield shouted. "You blundering idiot. I'm sending Able and Jones down right away to help you!"

He slammed down the phone and shouted at his secretary to get Lucia, who was in Los Angeles, on the phone. In a few minutes he spoke to her. "Have you heard the news of what's going on at Four Rivers?"

"I saw the papers this morning. Have been telling you for years to take care of those people for they've been looking for the least excuse to walk out!"

Whitfield silently cursed the pain in his heart. Losing money was more important to him than any health problem. "Something's got to be done fast before we lose that Navy contract and the strike spreads to our other plants!"

"I'm going there in a few days," she said. "I'll see what can be done. Meanwhile give them a decent wage scale and the proper fringe benefits. It's not Harvey Dodds' fault they're out on strike!"

He said scornfully, "Do what you can. But I see that you're batty about this Indian religious junk too!"

He hung up and stared at the traffic along the East River, then called his secretary to get the staff in the conference room at once. He sat there studying the skyline. Dodds could be a Red. Congressman Jack Rhey could subpoena him to appear before the House unAmerican Activities Committee.

Elsa Spain entered the office. "A special delivery package just came. From Murray Price. He mailed it from the West Coast just before taking off for India. Something about a deal you made with him over an ancient scroll. Wants you to let the Art Museum look at it, then give him an answer at New Delhi!"

"Crazy world," he snorted throwing the package in the file basket. "My best men running around the world gathering up junk. Wasting our time and money. Get me Jack Rhey at his Washington office. Then I've got to get into that meeting."

After several days in Four Rivers Lucia decided to leave for New York. She knew that the disorder in the town caused by the plant strike and Julie's condition were going to injure a lot of people.

Ben Carter, the plant manager at Four Rivers, was doing everything to put the blame on Dodds, and was being very successful at this too. Neither had the trouble shooters, Able and Jones, been able to do anything, and the Navy contract was gradually slipping away.

Whitfield was a successful man in making huge profits yearly for the Gatewood stockholders. He did this by locating the Gatewood plants in small towns where the local politicians would string along with violations of wage and fringe rights, especially in Four Rivers. The money he poured into the Four Rivers City Hall was meager in comparison with what he spent personally entertaining women and charging it up to his expense account.

The employees at the Four Rivers plant were far more underpaid than those engaged at other Gatewood plants throughout the world. Even the Unions had a tough time with R. J. and his bright boys.

Lucia left Four Rivers convinced that her father was going to make life hard for Harvey Dodds. If her suspicions were right there would also be a real showdown between herself and R. J., that meant more than a discussion of heated words. If necessary, she could give his story to her friends who worked for The Times. She knew that he beat the tax rap in 1952 by juggling the corporation's books and paying off the Federal agents. She had enough on him to put R. J. in Federal prison.

She had seen Harvey Dodds in Four Rivers and wondered if she were in love with him. The other problem that bothered her was Julie Vanners. Though the pretty, young girl had not told her the complete details she knew that R. J. was the culprit. This was quite a complex problem. She asked Julie to come to New York and stay with her, but the girl only said no, but she would consider it.

Upon arrival in New York Lucia went to her apartment and left her bags, then went downtown to the Gatewood offices on Fifth Avenue. R. J. Whitfield was there but he was plainly annoyed at the lack of her success with winning any of the strike leaders to his side. He was in a sharp, biting mood.

"I didn't go to Four Rivers to charm anybody," she said pointedly, "I couldn't do it anyhow. The whole town is against your scant wages and lack of benefits for the employees there. The only ones who benefit are the City Hall officials who take your money and do as they like.

"Give them a city hospital and let your employees and families have free treatment. Give them the same raise in salaries and benefits as in the other Gatewood plants."

"Did the trip give you a chance to see Harvey Dodds again?" he asked bitterly.

"We're talking about the plant," she held to the point.

"Why? Those people don't need much to live on. I lived on fifty dollars a week as plant manager in that town. Had a home and lived in style!"

"Things were far cheaper then. And that was mother's home you lived on," she said hotly, wondering if this were the time to talk about Julie Vanners. "You've dodged the problem too long at Four Rivers. Now you'd better pay your debts or lose your whole plant there. And that's something you can't afford to do. That Navy contract will give your stockholders a nice tidy little dividend this year. What are you going to tell the Board of Directors if you lose?"

"I run Gatewood!" he cried. "And I know what I'm doing. I'll keep that Navy contract and the Four Rivers plant going. They will bow to my demands!"

"You mean that you will starve those people down there, so you can show a greater profit on the books for your directors and stockholders!"

He glared at her while she pulled on her gloves smiling at his anger. She spoke again. "Your Four Rivers' employees are asking for bread while you plan a stone statue for yourself. They will love that. And maybe the government will like that idea of yours, in keeping a double set of books while showing them the set which gives a complete annual loss on the Four Rivers plant, and your stockholders the other one?"

He bellowed. "Did you get those ideas from that Dodds gang?"

"No! I talked with your chief accountant at the plant, R. J., and he is as sore as the rest of them. Why don't you get wise to yourself?"

His mouth flew open. "You're in love with that Harvey Dodds? That's the reason why you're making up those lies. You want to hurt me!"

She got up with tears in her eyes. "I'm in love with Harvey Dodds, if that is what you mean. But it doesn't do me any good. You ruined that years ago by starting that fight with his family."

"I'll fix him very soon," he growled. "There won't be any Harvey Dodds when I get through!"

"What are you up to R. J.?" she asked in alarm.

He smiled triumphantly. "There might be

a House unAmerican Activities investigation on your sweetheart. Jack Rhey is looking into the matter now. There might be evidence that Harvey Dodds is helping the Communist cause in America."

Harvey Dodds was extremely discouraged over the turn of events. No patients visited his office anymore. The population of the little town had turned against him because he had expressed his gratitude to those simple Indian people six thousand miles away for saving his life.

His nerves were jumping with alarming activity. His aunt, in her strong anger, had tried to sway him against Shyama, and had unwittingly revealed something he had long suspected. His father was really responsible for the death of Lucia's mother. R. J. Whitfield was right in his accusation.

He put his head in his hands and leaned against the desk. His thoughts ran riot. What a mess. How could Lucia have any thought of affection for him? She believed that R.J. was completely wrong about that event. How could he tell her.

For the first time he saw how money ruled the lives of these people, and the prejudices and strife in complete control of their minds, instead of the Light of God. Somebody had brought misery upon the Ghoshs by the theft of that manuscript. Was

Whitfield mixed up in this?

He felt willing to sacrifice everything to return to India and be with the *Mahanta, the Living ECK Master. To have just one more opportunity to gaze upon that powerful countenance of the one whom he had met in Allahabad called Viswapati—Lord of the World.

The nurse came into the office and announced that Julie Vanners was there. Straightening up he told her to send the girl in and stepped to the wash basin. He was drying his hands when she entered the office. For a moment he watched her wondering if this was the time to tell her. Did he have the courage? The thought went around in his head like a note of music in a tuba horn.

She looked peaked and worried. This bothered him but he greeted her cordially. "Sit here, Julie," he said arranging a chair for her alongside the desk. "I've got to tell you the truth!"

She smiled. "From the look on your face, Harvey, maybe I'd better try to cheer you up. You must have had a bad piece of news yourself."

"Let's talk about you, Julie," he said gently.

"I already know about myself, Harvey," she said folding her hands and dropping her glance upon them. "I really didn't need all your test tubes to tell me what was wrong."

"Have you discussed this with anyone

---

* Title given to Spiritual Head of ECKANKAR, the Light-Giver, the Vi-Guru, the Guru of all Gurus.

else?"

"Only you and Lucia when she was here. I haven't gotten up the courage to tell either father or mother. They'll die."

"I realize that!"

"Father will never forgive me. He's too straight laced. He'd be thrown out of his parish in disgrace. See what a situation I'm in, Harvey? I not only make myself miserable but do things which cause others trouble."

"Couldn't you go somewhere, Julie? There are lots of places."

"Lucia asked me to come to New York. I don't want to go. I couldn't impose on her." Tears began to drop down her cheeks. "I don't know what to do."

"Get hold of yourself, Julie. Won't Jesse Adams marry you?"

She shook her head. "No. It's not his affair!"

"Who is it, Julie?" he asked with the words jumbling through his brain.

"I can't tell you, Harvey!" she cried.

"Then what are you going to do, Julie? You can't stay here for everybody will know about it sooner or later. If you went to New Orleans or New York, word would get back. You've got to go further away than that!"

"I don't know what to do yet, Harvey. But I've got an idea that it will soon be over with!"

"What do you mean, Julie?" he asked in alarm.

"I don't think it's best for me to be around. I'm a complete disgrace to all including you."

Her eyes closed and the hair half-hid her pretty face.

He lifted her face with his hand under her chin and stared at her. Then the vision of the Master blotted out her face. "Get some sense in your head, Julie. You can't be talking like that. Why this is only a part of the giving of life to this world. Nature doesn't care how you give life as long as mankind reproduces its own species.

"It's going to be a hard struggle for a while but don't think of it in that light. Remember you are a mother and who the father is, at this point, doesn't count. You are to bring into the world something wonderful—a life."

"Harvey," she said softly. "Remember that night at the country club when I proposed to you?"

He nodded.

"I didn't mean it because of what has happened. I've always loved you Harvey. Ever since we were in high school."

"Julie! I'm not in love with you. To marry you now would not save the situation. Under the present circumstances I couldn't be a husband to anyone.

"Now listen. I've got friends on the west coast. Florence Kellogg heads a small sanitarium near Los Angeles. She is a good friend of mine, and would take care of you for as long as you want to stay. I will see that your expenses are cared for. Nobody will know you are there except Lucia and I. I am sure she would come to stay with you."

"It's no use, Harvey," she said rising from

the chair.

After she was gone he sat there thinking about the girl and her problem. He had a letter from Florence Kellogg the day before insisting that he come to the West Coast and work for her. She casually mentioned that there was a Tibetan Holy Man living somewhere close by in the mountains who was supposedly teaching ECKANKAR.

Shyama was unhappy about the events in Four Rivers. The loss of that manuscript was ever in his mind and there was the trouble for him with the college students since his date with Martha Long. Among the things which became very ridiculous was a rumor that spread among the social circles in town that Shyama was capable of great power which came from black magic or the evil forces of nature. Some called them the wickedness of Satan and wondered why Miss Carrie Dodds allowed him to remain in her home.

Mothers warned their daughters against Shyama. They believed that he was influencing Dr. Dodds in his stand for the art of ECKANKAR against his critics.

The words became a standing joke among the college students. Shyama had to defend himself several times on the campus and in the class room as the butt of vicious practical jokes. Many of the students would tease him unmercifully, ask if he would read their palms or did he have a crystal ball with him, or could he fly through the air without visible support.

The climax came when one of the school boys called Shyama a dirty name and told him that his religion was the world's great art of forgery. The boy's parents had discussed it in their home after Reverend Vanners denounced it from the pulpit as the work of the devil.

Anger exploded in Shyama's heart. He struck the boy and a fight started on the campus in which he was badly mauled, only to be saved by a passing policeman who delivered him, without gentleness, at the station house where Aunt Carrie Dodds, in the absence of her nephew, arrived in great flurry to bail him out.

When they got home she gave him a tongue lashing as he had never expected from anyone. His parents had never talked to him like that. He began to wonder if America was actually as wonderful as he had believed. Now he wanted to go home.

Harvey Dodds arrived at that moment. "What's the matter?" he said setting down his black bag and looking at the bruised boy.

"I just had to bail him out of jail for fighting. Get rid of him. He's caused you trouble enough!" she cried.

"Wait a minute," he said. "Let me hear his side of it."

Shyama's eyes were brimming as he whispered. "Somebody at school said something bad about the Master. I hit him and he hit me back!"

"Looks like he hit you more than you hit him!" Dodds grinned.

Shyama finished the story, "Now I want to go home!"

Aunt Carrie said sharply. "He's a disgrace, Harvey. Send him away!"

"I hear you, Aunt Carrie. I'll take him away in a few days. We'll find another place to live if he wants to stay with me."

"You would leave me, Harvey?" she cried. "After all I've done for you? You'd give up your inheritance for this?"

Harvey Dodds put his arm around the boy and led him into the bathroom. He turned at the door and spoke. "We'll talk about this later. However, remember this. I don't want your money, and Sammy has done nothing to harm either you or anyone else in town. It has been your own ignorance which has created the trouble."

"Wait a minute, Harvey!" she said firmly. "You're forgetting that I took you under my care after your father died in a drunken fit. If it hadn't been for me you'd followed in his footsteps and been a drunkard too. I kept you to the straight and narrow path!"

"You're overwrought, Aunt Carrie. Let's not talk about this now. Maybe tomorrow when we've had time to think things over!"

She cried. "You fool. You've inherited your father's lack of good sense. He ruined himself when attending Martha Whitfield at the time of Lucia's birth. He made a terrible mistake which cost him a practice and eventually his life!"

Terror rose sharply in Shyama as the man dropped his arm and faced the woman. They looked at one another with a terrible fire in their eyes. Then Harvey Dodds relaxed and with a face that was ashen gray, pulled the boy into the bathroom and seated himself upon a stool. He looked at the swollen eyes and bruised cheeks.

"Do I have to go home?" Shyama sobbed fretfully. "I didn't mean it when I said I wanted to leave you!"

"Not at all, Sammy," Dodds said, reaching for his medical kit. "That is up to you. You can stay with me as long as you wish. Do you understand that, Sammy? I love you dearly. But the choice is your own!"

Shyama swallowed hard. "I must try to find a way to get the manuscript back before returning to my parents."

He flinched as the open wound on his face stung from the antiseptic.

CHAPTER 6

The ringing of the telephone tore Harvey Dodds out of a sleep. He switched on the table lamp, reached for it and spoke into the receiver. The clock on the night table marked four a.m.

A woman's taut voice said, "This is Mrs. Vanners. Please come right away. Something has happened!"

Instinctively he said, "Is it Julie?"

"Yes!" Her voice was desperate. "Please hurry!"

He sprang out of bed and dressed hurriedly. As he went out the door, his thoughts were on the lack of hospital facilities in the town. He made it across town in a few minutes. The house was ablaze with lights. Mrs. Vanners still in her nightgown, hair disheveled and eyes red from weeping, ushered him in, and pointed mutely up the stairs.

He charged up the steps to the front bedroom and threw open the door. Julie was stretched out on the bed in light blue sleeping pajamas, like a small, white faced doll. She wore a half smile on her lips as though mocking the world. Her hands were folded over her breast giving her a serene expression. Cold, waxen fingers were the only expression of death about her. He would never forget those fingers. They reminded him of the everlasting flowers, always put on graves.

Reverend Vanners was kneeling beside the bed in prayer. He didn't look up when Dodds charged into the room. The physician dropped his bag wondering why they hadn't called another doctor since his ideas were in conflict with the minister's beliefs.

He felt for a pulse on the tiny hand but failed to locate it, then tried for heart action with his stethoscope. He finished the examination knowing it was useless to continue.

As he studied the package of sleeping tablets by the table, he wondered at R. J. Whitfield and his aunt, who could easily provide a hospital for the city, yet instead fought one another vying for honors in spending on parks, to be named after themselves or erecting dreary stone statues.

There were over twenty pills missing. Little wonder that she died. Rev. Vanners got up from the floor, breaking Dodds' chain of thoughts. He looked old and tired. "I got the tablets by prescription for my wife," he said wearily. "Julie must have found them!"

Dodds looked at the waterglass on the table. "When did you discover her?"

"Fifteen or twenty minutes ago. We heard her moaning. We found her lying across the bed but unconscious. We tried to call Dr. Vincent but he was out and then got you."

"Why didn't you call the fire department?" Dodds asked roughly. "They would have sent an emergency crew with a stomach pump."

"It was God's choice that she die," the minister said angrily. "Julie had sinned and for that the Lord took her away. I could do nothing for her."

"Can you be that callous?" Dodds asked bluntly.

"You knew about Julie's condition," the

man exclaimed, touching his hands together. "She had been consulting you."

"How did you know that?"

"Your nurse told me. And I'm quite aware of who is responsible for this situation. He must pay for it—the Lord will not let him go unrewarded for his wickedness. It was that heathen you brought here from India."

Shocked, Dodds stared at the man, then went down to the living room where Mrs. Vanners was waiting. "You'd better take care of the Reverend. I think he's overwrought."

"I know," she said wearily. "He will cause more grief unless I can talk him out of it. I'll telephone next week."

He left the house and drove to the office where he made out official papers on the girl's death, then rode along the waterfront looking at the river in the glow of dawn's brilliant colors. The Master would have an answer to this. Today he would write Swarachakraji and ask if he could return to India and live there at the ashram.

Lal Ghosh was surprised to get word to come to Nath Dwark's office immediately. He left the house wondering if this was his karma. The web of his karma had woven closely to Nath Dwark and all those who had passed through his life, all the tomorrows and into eternity until there was nothing more than God, the Absolute.

The spacious fields and snow-capped mountains that surrounded the little city were not in his consciousness as he reached the office and climbed the stairs to the second floor. Dwark was sitting behind his desk, his dark forehead in wrinkles and his big fists clamped in balls.

"I got your message, Dwark," Ghosh said in a husky voice. "I was anticipating it because your informer who was placed in my household as a servant broke under kind treatment and confessed about the plot you have for the return of my daughter. Do you wish to force me into some kind of political agreement?"

"It seems as if I'm caught in a trap of some kind instead of you, Ghosh." He spoke in a low rumbling voice that seemed to be on the edge of breaking. "You must understand that it is not I who is demanding the terms!"

Ghosh smiled with disbelief. "I am sincere. If you wish revenge for my part in the American's escape from India, then, I am willing to put myself in your hands. Provided my daughter is returned safely and you promise not to harm her again!"

"I can't promise you anything, Ghosh," the big man said sadly. "I've been told to make you come to political terms with me. You must believe that!"

"You're under orders?"

"The strictest orders which could be imposed on any man. Their plan is that you be ordered to place my name on the ballot at

— 111 —

the next election, replacing you for nomination for Mayorship. You are to act as my sponsor and will campaign among the members of the City Board for my election. It's a hard thing to tell you."

Ghosh paled. It meant the Communist party was making a supreme bid for the control of the city of Srinagar and if successful would become a strong political factor in the Province.

He said, "I see what you mean, so I am willing to follow out this plan provided my daughter is returned safely. I do this willingly and of my own accord, knowing what it means to my own career!"

"What does it mean to you, Ghosh?"

"That my reputation as an honest man in Kashmir will be ruined by the support I give you for public office from which I am retiring. My livelihood as an attorney-at-law will decrease, because the public will lose confidence in my judgment."

Dwark frowned. "This is what the Red chiefs meant for it to do. This is a part of their revenge." He pulled some papers from the desk drawer and pushed them at Ghosh. "Sign this. It's an agreement that you hereby give me public support as candidate for the office of Mayor at the next election."

Ghosh stared at the agreement. "This is not justice. Nothing in the document says that you will return my daughter!"

"What you say is the truth!" Dwark spoke bitterly. "But I didn't make out the agreement. I can't tell you if Amiya will ever come back or not! She is in Chung Ling's hands!"

"Chung Ling?" Ghosh echoed.

"Yes," Dwark murmured. "I had nothing to do with the kidnapping. He got her through force from my camp where she had been taken when the American Murray Price bribed one of my men to capture her. I would have sent her home except Ling got there first. My life is at stake unless you sign that agreement. I tell you that Ling wants the American and that manuscript back in India and will go to undue effort to get them. You have only a slim hope of getting Amiya back by signing that paper."

Ghosh knew it was a trick but he picked up the pen and wrote his name across the bottom of the paper.

Dwark said slowly, "You have my solemn promise that she gets back to you again!"

"As my enemy you are showing me a kindness. Why?"

Dwark replied, "Yes, I am your enemy. But I love your daughter. I never expect to have her as my wife, but my love is great enough to try to do something about her situation!"

Shyama's grief subsided. He heard Harvey Dodds enter the house, lock the downstairs door and come up the steps. A gentle rapping sound at the door and Dodds entered.

Shyama sat up in bed and switched on the table lamp. The man came across the room, silently, and sat down in a chair beside the bed, in the shadows beyond the rim of light. He lighted a cigarette and puffed on it.

"Something wrong?" the boy asked.

Dodds leaned over and took the boy's hand. "I see that you have been crying, Sammy. We will both miss her!"

Shyama whispered. "She was different. She was like a rose just coming into full bloom."

Dodds said quietly, "I want to ask you something personal, Sammy. Did you have any relations with Julie?"

The boy jerked up. His eyes went wide. "Of course not! There was nothing between us! Nothing at all! I loved her, yes. But not that way!"

Dodds crushed out the cigarette in an ash tray and paced the floor, with both hands behind his back. "Nobody but Julie, the nurse, her parents and myself knew why she took her life. But there is another person who hasn't yet been identified. I believe that I know who that person is."

He turned to the boy. "Julie took her life because she was going to have a baby. It would have been a disgrace to her family!"

"Upon my word before God," the boy whispered. "It was not me!"

"Rev. Vanners is half-crazy with revenge. He thinks that his daughter was the victim of foul play and somebody is going to pay for it." He stood looking at Shyama not wanting to tell him of the conversation between himself and Mrs. Vanners that morning. The woman had told him that Rev.

Vanners was planning a sermon for next Sunday to denounce the boy from the pulpit and try to stir the public enough to drive him out of the country!

He smiled cheerfully. "Don't let it bother you, Sammy. We will talk over things tomorrow!"

He went downstairs and called the Vanner's residence. The minister finally agreed to see him. The drive took only a few minutes and he was soon seated in the minister's study.

He said, "I've come to talk with you about this matter concerning my young Hindu friend. You are wrong if you believe that he had anything to do with your daughter's death!"

"I have proof, Doctor," the man said harshly. "There is little need for you to discuss this matter. It is absolutely useless to try to give me an argument. Absolutely useless!"

"I understand you are preparing a sermon on my friend, for Sunday?"

The minister stood up. "I intend to see that he is driven from the city. I will use every moral force possible against you for harboring him!"

Dodds flushed deeply. "I warn you to be careful in what you say on this matter." He got up. "Goodnight, Sir!"

"I urge you to send him away, Dr Dodds. For the good of all concerned before any further trouble develops."

Dodds said firmly, "You call yourself a Man of God! God never wants revenge. He gives love regardless of what has happened!"

When he got home there was a long distance call from Lucia Whitfield, in New York. She had gotten the news about Julie's death and wanted to know more. After he had finished she told him about her father's wrath piling up against the Dodds. R. J. Whitfield blamed Dodds' talk before the Four Rivers' Womens Club for the walkout at the local plant and loss of a Navy contract for two million dollars. R. J. was behind Rev. Vanner's drive to get Shyama out of the city, and there were plans for the House Unamerican Activities Committee to investigate Dodds for subversive activities. She concluded by saying that her father had a manuscript from India which she didn't know too much about.

Dodds hung up wondering if R. J. Whitfield engineered the theft of the manuscript. There was nothing further for either of them in this country and now it was best for them both to return to India. He went upstairs thinking that he and Shyama should go to New York and see Whitfield about that scroll.

Amiya stayed in the hut on the side of the mountain guarded by Ling's men. This evening she went outside to enjoy the cool mountain wind and the sunset, one of the few pleasures the Communist captors allowed her.

The mountain ranges frowned upon her with the glory of the golden light that spread in vast colors over the snow peaks. The scene was that of a fantastic world in which the earth was bathed in a panorama of colors.

She walked slowly looking at the sunset as Nath Dwark rode out of the trees toward her. Her heart beat too swiftly and she sucked in her breath hoping to slow it. He pulled up and dismounted from his iron-gray stallion.

Smiling he rubbed the stallion's neck and looked quietly at her. He said in a deep voice, "Good evening, Amiya Ghosh!"

"Have you come to take me home?" she asked hopefully.

He shook his great head. "I've been betrayed, little one. It seems that now Ling has struck a bargain and won a great victory. He isn't willing to fulfill the promises made to your father!"

"What promises, Nath?" she asked stepping close and putting a hand on his arm. She felt the warmth of his flesh and the shiver that ran through him.

"I saw your father yesterday, in the city. Ling forced me to make him agree to support me for Mayor in the next election. He was given the promise of delivering you home in good health. But the promise is broken!"

Horror grew in her heart. "You did that to my father?" she whispered.

He dropped his head with shame. "I did it because it was the only way to get you help. Ling threatened to kill you if I didn't.

I couldn't bear the threat. You see I'm in love with you, whether either of us like it or not!"

Feeling in her heart turned to soft tenderness that melted and ran together like a brook. Her eyes told him of the feeling. "Ah," she whispered. "How noble you are, Nath. Tell me about my father. How did he look?"

"Thinner, though greatly worried about you. I told him you are as well as could be expected under the circumstances. He sent his love and said they would be praying for your return as quickly as possible."

"My father has lived up to his part of the bargain. What more does Ling want? I'll go see him myself and demand that he return me to my home."

"Please, Amiya. Don't try to see Ling. Let me try to work it out some way."

"And risk becoming more involved with him," she said scornfully.

His hand caught her shoulder. "Do not try anything rash. I will do the best I can. I love you. Trust me. I will help you escape Ling some way or other."

She looked at him softly knowing this great Red chieftain loved her deeply. How could she understand anything else but love?

"I love you too, Nath Dwark, but what good does it do me. You are a Red and my father belongs to the party who hates your kind."

She felt his lips against her lips and the pain in her heart was sweet. Her arms went around him pulling him closer. Then suddenly they released each other and stepped back. She asked in a panting voice. "Why is Ling holding me?"

"He wants to force your father to make the American return to Kashmir with your brother and bring back the manuscript with them."

"How can he force my father to do that?"

Dwark muttered. "By threatening to murder you if Ghosh doesn't agree to it. If successful you will go home again!"

Harvey Dodds and Shyama arrived in New York later in the afternoon and went to a hotel on Park Avenue. Then Dodds caught a cab and went to the Gatewood Corporation offices hoping to find R. J. Whitfield there, but Elsa Spain would not let him see the President. He left in anger and frustration and rode across the town to Lucia's apartment hoping to find her home.

While the cab wove through the traffic he remembered something the Master had told him the last afternoon in the Ashram, talking about the subject of ECKANKAR. "The best way to get into your mind that you are an individual, walking around with your whole life in your hands, and that you are as much of the whole as a leaf on a tree is to realize this: the atmosphere, world, minerals, plants, flowers and human life is made up of the ECK Power. This pervading force is everywhere, in all. You cannot escape It. The cause of all manifestations you see in the world is from the fact that a Soul is like a radio or wireless station. You create and send out thoughts into the ether which is another part of the ECK Power. Your thoughts are picked up by another Soul to whom you may be sending and become a manifestation somewhere in this world, perhaps within your orbit of existence.

"You see we are the whole—of God itself, as some people want to call it. We are the leaves on the tree of God. As the whole we are never separate from one another but dependent upon the other for something, perhaps our economic life, maybe our emotional life and even the spiritual life. No person is alone. What I think, will be picked up by another, perhaps by my close disciples, or maybe somebody many hundreds of miles away.

"We are of the whole, dealing with the world on a basis of the whole being which is the ECK Power or whatever you want to call it—maybe love, God consciousness or another name. It is all the same.

"You are a part of me, and I am a part of you. We both are a part of everything and every individual in this world, including the worlds of minerals, plants and animals, yet we are ourselves each individuals.

"When you talk with another, it is the speaking with an extension of yourself. If angry, we are only angry with ourselves. We are like a mirror reflecting only what is within ourselves!"

His thoughts were cut short as the driver pulled up in front of a white-stone apartment house. The switchboard girl announced him and he went up to an apartment on the seventh floor. Lucia answered the door.

"Oh Harvey!" she exclaimed holding his hand. After they were seated she continued. "I suppose that you are here to bring about a showdown with R. J. It might go against you, fighting him, instead of staying away. I don't know how you are going to accept my part in this for after all I'm his daughter whether I like his personal ethics or not."

He smiled. "Go ahead. I'm listening!"

"I don't take too well to what father is doing to you. But I am still a Whitfield and you might turn your complete hatred on me if R. J. succeeds."

"You're right about the reason I'm here. As your relationship stands, I pretty well judge things upon their merits from a reasonable standpoint, not from an emotional basis."

"What do you want me to do, Harvey?" she asked ringing for the maid and ordering coffee.

"I came to New York to find out if R.J. has a parchment in his possession which belongs to the Ghosh family. You mentioned it the time we talked the other day, on the phone when you called about Julie. Does R. J. really have it?" Then he gave the history of the scroll and why it was in America.

She looked at him curiously. "I really don't know too much about it, except Elsa Spain mentioned it one day and asked what it was all about. Seems that Murray Price was responsible for it getting into R. J.'s hands. But Father must not have realized the actual bargaining power of it!"

"I must get my hands on that manuscript, Lucia," he declared. "It belongs to Shyama's family. Although they are wealthy, the money would help at this point. Will you help me?"

"Yes," she said looking at him tenderly. "But I think you're going at it in the wrong way. If you could get to R. J. and try to make a deal with him, he would instantly be aroused and start an investigation which would end up by putting him on top with a handful of aces!"

"What can I do?"

She said, "I'll handle it, Harvey." Then paused. "Not to change the subject but do you understand my motive for helping you?"

He shook his head slowly watching her with wide, gray eyes. Somewhere in his mind was a thought the Master had left with him. The heart was the most sensitive spiritual faculty of the body. One felt with the heart. Therefore, the heart revealed what lay beyond the power of reason to ascertain. Truth could be revealed immediately in a pure heart. The heart responded always directly to truth; therefore, its knowledge was always intuitive. He pulled himself up with a start. Why was he thinking about that?

He said, "I believe you don't want R. J. to

push anybody around as he has tried with me. You have a sense of justice that won't let you!"

"Is that what you believe?" she asked, rising as the white skirt flared outward around her slender legs. "Is it Harvey?"

Her perfume got into his brain and made him dizzy. "I'm dodging, Lucia!" he said. "You're aware of it. You're in love with me, but really I don't know what to say!"

"Was it Julie?" she asked. "Are you the father of that baby?"

"No, for both questions. I don't know who the father is. The woman I marry will have my complete love!"

She put both her arms around his neck and said softly, "May I have your complete love?"

He groaned, "I'm confused."

"Is it Amiya Ghosh?"

He laughed nervously. "You want to get to the bottom of this?"

"I want the truth, Harvey," she said firmly.

"I wondered about Amiya. She's a beautiful girl and stays in my mind, but we couldn't marry. We are just different people. I belong here. Even Sammy suffers from not being at home with his family."

She looked at him a long time. "I don't have a chance with you, Harvey?"

"Look Lucia,' he said. "I came to talk about the manuscript. Now let's put it this way. Let's don't see each other for a while. You try to get the manuscript for Sammy. I'll have him get in contact with you."

"You are going to leave New York?"

"I don't know, Lucia. You and I are not for each other. I'll go to California soon to start a practice out there, maybe with Florence Kellogg in Los Angeles."

"I should have followed my intuition and not seen you. You think I'm trying to trick you!"

"You're R. J.'s daughter!" he exclaimed sharply, turning to go.

"What you're thinking isn't true!"

"I can't trust myself, Lucia," he said sadly. "I'm sorry but I can't!"

"You can't win by running away. Go back to Four Rivers and face it out with everybody. Be a man, Harvey."

He turned and looked at her, eyes shining. "I don't have the guts, Lucia. Not after learning the truth. My aunt told me that R. J.'s right in this family quarrel. It is true what he accuses my father of doing; of killing your mother. Now I haven't even got the nerve to see you again!"

He slammed the door behind him.

The Reds in Kashmir revealed their hand too soon in the Srinagar elections campaign by letting out the news that Nath Dwark would be sponsored by Lal Ghosh for the office of the Mayor.

Dwark was staying away from the city aware that Ling had made a mistake in doing this. His guess on the reaction of the public was correct. The people didn't like it but there was little they could do. They blamed Ghosh for their predicament, and were suspicious of everything that went on within the political circles.

Ghosh watched with a sadness in his heart knowing that the Reds had outwitted him. He had received, instead of his daughter's return, a demand that he send for his son to return to India with the parchment and make an appeal for the American to come back also, or Amiya would be murdered.

He got up early this morning and prepared to go to the office, his thoughts upon the Master, of the time they were together walking along a road near the Ashram. It was years ago, before he was married.

The blue and gold of the morning under the ancient sun of India had filled him with such joy he could hardly contain himself.

Suddenly he burst out with a question. "Master! What is God?"

The Master's luminous eyes turned upon him with a sweeping gaze. The sage lifted his hand and pointed at the wide, vivid blue sky stretching across the vast horizons. The boy's mind saw, felt and loved.

They walked onward through the rustling green forest where the sunlight was a sweet, cool pattern upon the earth. He looked around again and felt the rush of peace and harmony in his heart. He asked again, "Master! What is God?"

The Master smiled lovingly and pointed again at the long aisles of majestic trees.

Ghosh remembered that he looked and thought that he had seen nothing.

They came out of the forest and followed the long, white highway over the green hills and met the gypsies singing gay songs of the road. A mother went by carrying a child in her arms that gurgled and laughed as the sun struck its brown face. He felt the love of the child filling his Soul. Ghosh had asked again. "Master! Tell me what is God?"

The Master had turned to him with great compassion in his eyes. "My son, you have asked three times what is God? Yet three times you have seen God. Each time I showed you God, but you saw IT not, so I must interpret God for you!"

He smiled gently. "God is the sky which I showed you; the trees in the forest and the smiling face of the child. God is all, in everything and everywhere! But the greatest secret of all—is this. God is the love you experience in your mind, feel in your heart and know in yourself. Did you not love the blue of the sky with your mind when I showed it to you? Did you not experience the peace in your heart in the forest? And did you not feel the love of the child in your heart? You did and you knew God, you are Soul, and therefore a part of the divine SUGMAD!"

Ghosh dismissed the memories from his mind. After breakfast he left the house with one of his servants to reach the office before the day's activities began.

Half-smiling to himself about his memories with the Master, he walked through the crowd which was moving to the early market place to buy fresh meats and vegetables for the day. He was startled out of his reveries by a disturbed vibration around him. Looking up he saw the faces of the people staring at him with viciousness in their eyes.

Alarm arose sharply in him for he had seen that expression on the faces of a mob many times. They were making a demonstration against him for his stand in the Municipal Board elections.

They shouted at him and moved in quickly. He tried to escape but they trapped him in a circle. A stone struck his forehead, causing sharp pain. He jerked backwards and tried to beat his way through the crowd but they packed themselves in around him tightly. He managed to push to the outer circle when the police arrived and drove back the crowd, then escorted him safely home.

He went into the house tearfully seeking out his wife. She was in her bedroom for it was seldom she went anywhere since her daughter had been taken away.

He told her what had happened and then went to bed as she sent for the physician who arrived within a few minutes. The doctor looked over Ghosh and said, "He has a bad bruise on his temple. Give him complete rest for a few days. Feed him in bed. I'll be back tomorrow!"

Late that night when the household was quiet Lal Ghosh slipped from his bed and went to the little family altar where he prayed for strength to make a decision about his son. When he arose he knew that nothing else could be done than to write Shyama and tell him the predicament in which the family was and Amiya's captivity. He would order Shyama to return and bring the manuscript with him.

However, the real problem was how to get Captain Harvey Dodds to voluntarily return to India. How could it be done?

CHAPTER 7

Bhola Lal Ghosh was amazed at his own lack of responsiveness to his troubles. He was like a helpless child in face of some apparent danger in facing the enemy. This was in reverse to his behaviour in the past when he could handle himself with deft ability and skill. Some psychological mechanism had gone wrong. A deep subtle force which had been working up through the recesses of his brain and Soul had turned from that channel of confidence and skill into a path of failure.

He laid it to fear for the safety of his daughter.

The inertia within him surprised and stunned his conscious mind. He had no weapons with which to fight this trouble. God seemed to have left him and the appeal through prayer gave little relief. Tragedy had seized him so strongly that he could no longer do his spiritual exercises of ECK.

Small boys broke the windows in his house with stones. They wrote threatening words in chalk on the house walls. He knew that this was instigated by their parents.

Finally Ghosh decided to lay the trouble before his Master, and writing a note to his wife, early in the morning slipped out of the house, caught the express for Punjab where he changed trains and arrived in Kumur late that afternoon.

The people of the Ashram greeted him joyfully. The atmosphere took the strife and turmoil out of his heart. He found the Master sitting before the door of his hut with a number of his chelas.

The Master rose from his seat, with a wonderful smile, and came forward to greet Ghosh. The aura of the Master's love reached out and touched Ghosh and gave him that marvelous peace for his Soul. At once Ghosh felt safety in the arms of God again.

Swarachakraji dismissed the disciples and motioned for Ghosh to come into the hut where they seated themselves on straw mattresses and sat in silence for a while.

Finally the Master spoke in a deep reverent voice. "My son, you have been torn with grief over the problem of your daughter's absence in the enemy's hands. You were not wise in giving in to the will of Ling. The people of Srinagar do not like it, as you have come to know. By turning from God, the forces within you have been diverted into the Kal (negative) channel. You have come to ask my advice of what you should do."

Ghosh was not surprised at the knowledge which the Master possessed of his troubles. In fact he was aware that this wonderful man knew everything. Swarachakraji could easily read his thoughts although it was seldom that he spoke to anyone about this especially his own chelas, unless they first approached him. He considered Soul and Its aspects to be a house and unless invited into that house it was not good to try to force his way through the door.

Ghosh answered. "Yes, Master. I must

know the answer. I am the shell of the man I once was. No longer do I try to practice the goodness as you taught me. I can do nothing. I sit and brood constantly. If only I could get to my office and try to work. I cannot get over my grief for Amiya's disappearance. Has the ECK turned against me?"

"The ECK is not against you nor any member of your family." The Master spoke in the voice like the whispering of the wind in the trees. "This is a part of your doings. Your own actions have brought about this deed. You alone are responsible for your actions. If you had taken the action of the prit (positive) path when the brigand chief demanded you sign that agreement there might have been a lesser evil. You did not take the right action. Fear rules you instead of love.

"You must understand, my son, that while you are dwelling in the three worlds, that which consists of matter, energy, space and time, you are subjected to an exact payment for everything that is done—known to you as karma. You assisted the American to escape from India; therefore, the compensation must be made for that deed. Your family was caught up in the mesh. The law of God, in the lower worlds is to the point. There is little difference in its payments for the Great Soul does not care how it is to be done, but is compelled to act under the very nature of its own being.

"Thus God works in the three worlds— works as compensation. In every experience be it painful or otherwise, there is a compensation power to be gained or a reward which is well worth the suffering necessary to build it into soul-growth. This is also the great law of the lower worlds, but not that of the real Kingdom of Heaven.

"There is written in the book of St. John, 'A woman when she is in travail hath sorrow because her hour is come; but as soon as she is delivered of the child, she remembereth no more the anguish for joy that a man is born into the world.'

"In the lower forms of life, of any life in the material worlds, the law says an eye for an eye and a tooth for a tooth. This was the law that early ECK Masters had to teach the people for they were not evolved to the point whereby they could advance by the more subtle law of Love. Then came another who taught that by the law of Love we could overcome all things.

"That which makes up our lives in this world is the result of cause and effect, and which we call karma. It is the effect of causes set up in other times or former lives, which are brought to us in orderly sequence to be worked out and in turn set up better causes for our lives in the future. The idea I am trying to get across to you for understanding is that karma is neither a reward nor punishment for past deeds, and still less the avenging angel which the old scripture writers described to us. It was never this, for those writers had to use an overexaggeration in order to impress a race of people who had far less understanding than today to keep them in order for one another.

"We must have this law in the lower worlds simply for the purpose that the effect of our causes bring to the Soul the opportunity to learn certain lessons which It has not learned in a past life, hence, the law of Love brings it through this manifestation that it may gain soul-quality for further progress."

"What is the lesson that this brings me, Master?" asked Ghosh.

"The lesson of faith, my son. Your efforts to protect your family from evil by cooperating with evil shows that your faith is greater in that force than in God. As result of this you are sunk to the lowest ebbs of your misery. This is the result of the previous action in which you believed in evil and now it has returned to you. When you give up this idea completely and believe fully in God your problems can be overcome."

"What shall be done, Master?"

"Nobody can straighten out the wrong in yourself but you. You have that power and should make up your mind to do so."

"But will that bring Amiya back again?"

"It will. Remember this. He who manifests faith or love in God, does not do it with God, but as one working with God, and the attitude of the mind is born of this realization. In other words, all men are the channels of the divine power and must work as that channel and not with the channel.

"Everything in our lives within the material world is based upon three things: choice, imagination and willpower. By choice we must make up our minds to take a certain course of action; by imagination we must establish the ideal of God within ourselves and third, we must hold to this mental image of the ideal by our will power." The Master finished by saying, "I will not interfere in anyway with the law of God. My power is limited to myself. You must be willing to fulfill the law of God!"

Ghosh left the Ashram with the thoughts whirling through his head. He did not understand the Master. Now the Guru had refused to help him in his worst crisis. Was He really a Godman? Perhaps he was mistaken in his belief in Swarachakraji. Perhaps he was not the living Master after all and did not have any powers.

R. J. Whitfield was in Washington to see the Navy officials about the contract which was now gradually slipping from his hands at the Four River's plant. He was making some progress but decided at the end of the day to see Congressman John B. Rhey, whom he was responsible for putting into Congress, and who was now working on the investigation of Harvey Dodds.

He went to the House of Representatives and was ushered into the Congressman's private office. He entered, head high, playing the part of the dynamic captain of industry. He was a success in the business and industrial world, at the top of the ladder. Many of his friends in the same position had committed suicide over financial entanglements, losses and problems but he was aware that this would never occur in his life.

Jack Rhey was a small, baldish man, with horn-rimmed glasses. He jumped up from his desk and grabbed Whitfield's hand, but winced at the forceful pumping this industrialist gave him.

Whitfield smiled, secretly proud of his powerful hand grip. "You're in the pink of condition."

"Not me, but you!" said the Congressman. "I'd give you a million dollars for the secret!"

Whitfield felt himself swell with pride seeing the man grovel before him. He took out two slim cigars and passed one along to the Congressman and lighted his own from a silver cigar lighter. "Imagination, Jack. There's a better name for it. Creativity! That's all there is to it. Everybody knows it, but how many people actually use that part of their brains. The reason why people think that guys like us have got the secret formula is because we do three things; make up our minds to do a job; put our imagination to work, and use our willpower to keep it going. Simple, isn't it?"

He paused, puffed on the cigar. "Now every captain of industry, like myself, cannot build a giant corporation which may coordinate hundreds of smaller firms and thousands of employees, and utilize millions of dollars in capital funds until he has first created the entire work in his imagination. Objects in the material world are as clay in a potter's hand. It is in God. Oh yes, I believe in God as much as the preacher does, but in a different way. That the real things are created by man himself and that they are done so by creating.

"Are you aware of the fact that I have put in hours of playing games in my mind for the building of Gatewood before it came into actualization of being the great organization that it is? Well, so much for that. Let's get down to the reason why I stopped in to see you Jack."

"Is it about Dr. Harvey Dodds, R.J.?"

Whitfield nodded briefly. "The fact is that he might be working with subversive elements in this country is of little interest to me, Jack. But you know as well as I, that I am only looking to the welfare of the nation. I was in Washington, and thought it would be best to stop in and see what you had done about the case."

"Glad you did, R. J. Now we can get down to some brass tacks about it."

Whitfield said, "Here's the way I see it. I've been watching what the lad's been doing down at Four Rivers. Mind you I like the boy personally and helped him get out of India when the Reds were about to catch up with him and slam him back in prison. But when he got home he just went haywire and started preaching that doctrine which had been so hard on him. It sure played havoc with my plant and made me lose a couple million dollars in Navy contracts."

He puffed on his cigar. "You know the facts of the case. What have you done about investigation procedures?"

The Congressman squirmed and leaned back looking directly at Whitfield. "Nothing," he said flatly. "I had some investigators down there for a couple of weeks but they didn't find out anything wrong, R.J. I couldn't prove a thing if we put that man on the witness stand!"

The cigar almost fell out of Whitfield's mouth. "What?" he roared. "You mean to say that after all that trouble down there you can't prove a thing on Harvey Dodds?"

"Nothing, R.J.!" said the man. "If you want to pull up any facts the only thing they could use is that Dodds is crazy about some strange religion called ECKANKAR. We would get in a lot of hot water for that. Every newspaper in the country would ridicule us. We would become the laughing stock of the nation. Why they'd even have a Swami on the witness stand with a crystal ball."

Whitfield sat up straight staring at the Congressman.

Rhey swallowed hard. "Besides he belongs first to the Air Force. If there is any truth in what you're saying then he would have to be court-martialed before we could do anything about it."

Whitfield's hand slammed the desk. "My Lord!" he bellowed. "You're a dope, Jack. And I warn you to find out yourself. Are you scared that this will take you out of Congress? If you don't put that guy on the

— 137 —

witness stand right away I'll have you scalped. You'll be the laughing boy of Four Rivers. You'll walk the streets looking for a job!"

Grabbing his hat and brief case he stomped out of the office chewing savagely on his cigar.

Shyama got up that morning after Harvey Dodds had left the hotel to find a letter from his father forwarded from Four Rivers. Before he touched it, his mind told him that something was wrong. It had an aura that seemed to vibrate trouble. He had known for a long time that something was wrong in his home in India. There was normally a rapport between him and his sister which was easy for attunement as a form of mental telepathy. However, since arriving in America there had been no inner communication with her. He was growing uneasy about matters at home, knowing that his father had not written at all.

He tore open the envelope. His intuition proved to be right. There was trouble in Srinagar for his family, and Amiya was missing. The letter told him everything.

He put the letter aside and laid down on the bed, his face in the pillow. His mind was stunned. After a while he started sobbing quietly. His father had told him all and asked that he come back home and bring the manuscript with him. The letter was in confidence, and told him that unless

Harvey Dodds could be persuaded to return to India, Amiya would not be sent home by her kidnappers.

He sat up wondering what explanation could be made to Harvey to get him back to India. If he told Dodds the truth, a serious problem might be created. The American might refuse flatly. If he tricked Dodds into doing it, the deed would be on his conscience forever.

Filled with misery he pocketed the letter and left the hotel, going out on the street hoping the air would help him work out things in his mind. He did not know what to do, but if he had to return home without that manuscript his mind had to be prepared to inform his father that it was missing.

He loved the colorful crowds in the American cities but this time he walked along Fifth Avenue in the masses of people feeling for the first time completely apart from them. He had always been in unity with these strange Americans, even though they did not accept him as one of themselves. In this great cosmopolitan city there was an atmosphere of friendliness which was more to his nature than the little town of Four Rivers where most of the people seemed to resent him.

He strolled along the street looking into the windows of the shops hoping to take his mind off his problem, yet not seeing anything but his family and their sorrows in his home at Srinagar. Suddenly he realized that he was thinking about Julie Vanners.

He shook it off and put his thoughts back to his own problems. He was torn deeply between his debt to the American who was now as much his own brother as anyone could be. But he also owed a loyalty to his family. He knew, however, that his duty lay with his father, mother and sister, and that in the time of a crisis he should rush to them ready to help wherever possible. Now when the great test had come and he was called to return to Srinagar to help he was not able to.

He walked along in the brilliant sunlight of the late morning thinking that it was best for him to stay in America at the present time. This was wrong, of course, but it was the putting off of a problem that might be solved by his father's next letter.

Passing a church he looked inside at the dark, cool benches, then decided to go in and sit in silence and contemplation.

He sat there quietly for a long time remembering that years ago, as a child of nine, he had sat under a tree with the Master who talked about love. Childlike he asked the Master what love was?

The Godman smiled graciously. "Love," he said gently, "is the greatest and most sublime force of the universe. Through love the divine qualities of the SUGMAD shine like the radiant light of the morning sun, my child.

"When love enters into your heart, all gravitates to the inspiring beauty which it radiates. To serve and cherish love, as the ideal, is as unquestionable as the tender fragrance of the lotus flower.

"Love inspires the heart first as human love, that love which desires to serve its closest; husband, wife, children, family, friends, or human ideal, during this life's existence. But when the heart becomes refined by selflessness it evolves to divine love.

"Divine love is the noblest quality of God. Loving and serving God through every universal agency unfolds divine love. The heart so permeated by divine love becomes purified. Through divine love the heart surmounts every obstacle to become firmly established on the path of God.

"Your heart must willingly aspire to serve God through love. By this joyful performance the heart fulfills God's great principle of love, and becomes known to all as the loving heart. Through the loving heart only does the Soul attain immortality, my child.

"That, and that alone, Shyama, little one, is what love is."

Shyama opened his eyes and saw that standing close was the figure of the Master who smiled at him. He put out a hand then drew it back as the white outline of the Godman faded into nothingness.

He rose hurriedly and went back to the hotel hoping to find Harvey Dodds there. His mind was made up to stay with the American although his heart was filled with misery over his sister.

Dodds returned to the hotel to find the boy gone. He laid down on the bed awaiting Shyama's return. After a while the lad came in and took a chair. Dodds sat up and lit a cigarette.

"Something wrong, Sammy?" he asked casually dropping the match into an ashtray.

"I had a letter from home today," the boy said explaining what had happened but left out the details of his sister's kidnapping and the request to get Dodds back to India. "But I've decided to wait for a little while. If news doesn't get better then I will return to my family for that is all I can do."

"I agree with you, Sammy," Harvey Dodds replied warmly but feeling curious over the fact that Ghosh had ordered the manuscript to be returned. "However, the decision is your own to make. I ask that you do not let our friendship stand in the way. I know you belong there in the time of trouble."

"I will not let our friendship stand in the way, Harvey," the boy said tactfully.

Harvey Dodds paced the floor with a worried expression on his thin countenance. "I wish there were something that we could do. I came to New York hoping to get my hands on that parchment but it looks like we will have to wait a little longer. Do you think that your parents would come to America if I arrange for it?"

The boy shook his head. "No. I don't think so. Let us wait for a little while and perhaps the trouble will blow over."

"I had a letter from a friend in California who runs a clinic just outside the city of Los Angeles. She has been trying to get me out there for years to work with her. She asked me to join her staff. I got an idea that while we are waiting to hear about that scroll that we could run out there and have a talk with her.

"There is nothing that can be done with R. J. Whitfield in New York. According to Lucia, who is going to help us, the old man has lost some of his zeal for persecuting me or had other interests. She is looking for the manuscript. Meanwhile, we will look at that job and if I want to take it you can enter college out there and finish your education."

The boy nodded.

They boarded a plane the next day for California. Harvey Dodds settled back in his seat comfortably, thankful to be getting away from New York.

After a while he turned to the boy and asked, "Sammy, tell me what does the Master do to spiritualize the body? I mean how does He go about getting Soul ready for entering into the cosmic consciousness?"

Shyama was silent for a long time then finally said. "You are speaking of the liberation of Soul, Harvey. The best way I remember what the Master has said goes something like this. Within man are the worlds of God, and they are all under the control of the ECK power, which is also the individual expression for the unfoldment of the spiritual consciousness into the perfection of the Soul, and the universal self.

"Many views have been given the heavens within man, which the spiritual founders of religions, and mystics, have reached in their journeys into the cosmic worlds.

"The Master's teachings show us how to enter into these cosmic worlds daily through meditation, with the radiant body, the Atma Sarup of the Master.

"The first division, at the top of the worlds, is Sat Desh. It consists of several planes grading downward. The first of these is the highest where dwells God, the Supreme Being, who is pure spirit, unmixed with matter of any sort, and free from imperfection. Only pure spirit dwells here.

"The lowest of these divisions is Sach Khand where dwells the first manifestation of God in body form. He is called Sat Nam.

"Next is the Second Grand division called Brahmanda, the middle division. It is a very high order of creation, mostly spiritual, but mixed with mind and other very fine sorts of matter. This is the home of the Universal Mind, or prana. All Souls in their descent from Sach Khand stop here to take on mental apparatus for the purpose of contact with the worlds below and vice versa.

"The heavens of all the worlds' great religions are located here. This is the heaven of the Brahmands. Here dwells, as ruler, a deity called Maha Kal, and the land is known as Brahmanda, and Par Brahm. It is vast in area when compared with the physical universe but small beside the first Grand Division. It is subdivided into many distinctive regions or planes.

"These subdivisions shade into one another so imperceptibly that it is not easy to say just where one ends and another begins. This accounts in part for the many descriptions of those regions, and the great variety of names assigned them by various religions.

"Anda is the lowest of the heavens. It lies nearest the physical earth, and its capital is called Sahasra dal Kanwal, meaning thousand petalled lotus. Its name is taken from the great cluster of lights which is the actual power house of the physical universe.

"Millions of the earth's former great people of all ages of history are living a happy life here. This is the first station on the upward path of ECK. It forms a port of entry for all the higher regions for those traveling to still higher planes. Although life here has great longevity, the region is not immortal for after billions of years it is wiped out and there follows a period of darkness equal in duration to its life. Then a new creation is started and once more it lives as before.

"The Souls who inhabit this world are drawn into the higher worlds, at the time of dissolution, in a comatose state, to be replaced again on those worlds when they are ready for habitation.

"The fourth Grand Division, beginning from above, is called Pinda which is that including the physical world. Here coarse matter predominates, there being a small percentage of mind and still smaller amount of spirit. Our earth is a small and insignificant part of this grand division. Pinda extends far out into space beyond the reach of any telescope.

"In this lowest of all divisions of creation there is but little light and sound, and very low grade life, when compared with Brahmanda. This is the negative pole of light and spirit.

"As a rule the inhabitants of one plane are wholly unconscious of all other planes below or above. They live and die somewhat as we do and pass on to other regions as their karma impels them.

"It is quite evident that the spiritual traveler knows of all life throughout the universes but will not openly discuss it for the reason of not shocking man, nor to be taken for a fool, because man cannot see through the physical veil.

"The Master will gradually lift up the Soul to the planes, so as not to shock it from too much exposure to the spiritual rays of the higher worlds. After all, it is really not a movement of any kind except in the sense of the consciousness. We are in the center of eternity—here and now—how can we go anywhere?"

He finished and they sat in silence.

After a while Harvey Dodds said, "That

was some profound speech you just made. How did a seventeen year old boy learn all that and remember it?"

"It has been drilled into me since birth. I can remember it when needed at the right time. When the right time comes for you to be given initiation into the ECK, the glories and wonders of God will be for your own experience. I cannot tell you in words about them!"

CHAPTER 8

Harvey Dodds and Shyama settled themselves in a small cottage in a surburban area near Los Angeles; however, Dodds failed to come to any decision about joining the staff of the Kellogg clinic.

Late one evening he was getting ready for a party at Florence Kellogg's when Shyama came into the house and stood in the doorway of the bathroom watching him shave.

The boy said wistfully, "Just a little lonesome for company. Want to be with you for a few minutes. Gosh, but this is a big country, this California. And there is no prejudice against me at school!"

"I'm glad to hear about that, Sammy. I have been thinking very seriously about taking that offer from Florence Kellogg to settle down here. Just one thing I can't understand. What's wrong with my mind? I don't seem to understand why I keep hesitating to make the move!"

"Perhaps it's the Master. You know there are times when he won't let you do something because it doesn't fulfill your duty to him. In case you don't know it by now, I'll tell you. You've been under his protection ever since you entered India with the Kazakhs. He watches over the lives of His own people. And you're one of them."

Harvey Dodds washed the lather off his face. "That's a new theory for me. How about all of us? Like Lucia and any of

— 148 —

those who have accepted his teachings but never have been initiated?"

"You are all under his protection," Shyama replied. "Say, what are you getting dressed for? Going some place tonight without me?"

Dodds wiped his face with a towel and grinned. "I'm going to a party at Florence Kellogg's. Didn't think you'd be interested, but come along if you wish!"

"I don't think so. The ways of the Occidentals at parties are beyond my understanding."

Dodds laughed. "I know what you mean. I'll be late in getting home tonight."

He left the cottage and went out to the car. Since their stay in California he had purchased a second hand automobile. California was a land where great distances had to be traveled for the nearest errand.

That offer at the Kellogg clinic appealed to Dodds. He had had several conferences with the woman about accepting a place on her staff. She had needed a skilled surgeon for a long time and the trouble which Whitfield was trying to create for Dodds did not bother her. She laughed about it, and said the publicity would help her business. Everybody in Southern California was publicity conscious and this was a place where he could talk ECKANKAR to his heart's content. All people there were in some cult or other. Yet he could not make up his mind. Something deep within him, far down from any point of contact was pulling him away from all that was formerly dear to his heart.

He drove out to the home of Florence Kellogg which was perched in the hills overlooking Hollywood. The drive took almost an hour and this gave him a chance to do some thinking. His thoughts were mostly on what had happened to Lucia since they had quarreled in New York. She had disappeared from sight, and nobody knew where she was. She had promised to help recover the manuscript.

The party was in full swing when he got there. A three man string orchestra was playing sweet music. Quite a number of people greeted Dodds although he was not sure he knew them.

Florence Kellogg, a breezy western girl about thirty-five, who had been a nurse and had met Harvey at the New York Medical Center when he was doing his internship, came forward to greet him.

She introduced him to the guests then took him into a dining room where a buffet supper was being served and sat with him while he ate. A large number of guests had already eaten and were sitting on a broad verandah, in the rear of the house which overlooked Hollywood, Los Angeles and the suburban towns down to the sea.

Harvey Dodds and his hostess joined the group and watched the soft twilight settle over the landscape, and the twinkling lights of the valley below were almost the reflection of the stars in the blue bowl of heaven.

In response to the general request of the group Dodds told about his life in the Chinese prison and in India; then his escape from both locales, and of his desire to explore the teaching of Soul Travel—especially of his strong urge to return to India once again to see the Living ECK Master.

"The ECK mystical life is a strange one," he said. "It is not at all comparable with the way of living in the West. While we, in the West search for the manifested form in materials or the outer world, depending on these things for meaning, judging the success of our neighbor by his possessions—the devotee of the Master searches the worlds within himself for enlightenment.

"I've been told that in the initial states of God the devotee's consciousness merges with the cosmic spirit, and in this state he becomes a co-worker with the Universal Reality. This is so abstract that I am not sure whether it will work or not; however, I have become so fascinated by the procedure that it will not leave my mind alone."

Florence Kellogg said, "What is the greatest feature of this teaching as you see it, Harvey?"

"The Sound Current," Dodds replied. "It is the true science of the Masters who have come to earth in all ages to teach this science to men. We are never without a true

Living ECK Master. Every individual in the world must seek the path for himself and walk upon it himself, alone, except for the Master. The Master is the only one who can accompany him. You must have a living Master for he can act as the transformer to light the spark within to start the search for God.

"The sound current is the basic aspect for all religions. It is often called the Audible Life Stream and this is the cardinal, central fact in ECKANKAR, known as the Science of Soul Travel. It is what distinguishes this teaching from all other sciences or systems. It is the one sign by which a genuine Master may be recognized. And no one can be a genuine Master unless he teaches and practices the Audible Life Stream.

"This current is the ECK Power, Love, or what you might call the ECK Consciousness. It is the 'Word.' It is a stream, a life giving, creative stream, and it can be heard. The fact that it is audible is extremely important, and the idea of any system that applies a name to it shows that teaching to know of its importance.

"This current or wave contains the sum total of all life emanating from God. It is God in expression, and it is ITS method in making ITSELF known to all.

"The Word of God is called many names: The Voice of Silence; the Voice of God; the Music of the Spheres; Nada in Hindu, or Shabda Dun, the melodious sound. Often it is called Akash Bani which means heavenly utterance. The Muslim Saints call it Sultanul-Askar, meaning the King of the Ways.

"In a sense it is not a sound for it cannot be heard by the physical ear. It is audible only to the spiritual ear which is attuned to its higher vibrations. In the West it is that divine Logos known as the lost word.

"This creative current may be likened to the electro-magnetic waves of a radio, filling all space. The receiving set is the Soul within man. As soon as the living Master tunes in on this current and shows the way of keeping that tune-in then the entire body, and its mind and other subtle bodies must be cleansed and purified, then attuned to the higher vibrations.

"When we are ready to die, it becomes very easy for us to throw off the physical body and under the Master's guidance, ascend this divine wave to God."

A woman asked, "If the tuning in to the divine sound has got you nothing but misery since you have returned from India, then why do you spend all this time searching? For what purpose does it serve your life?"

Dodds smiled. "I have not yet come to the techniques of practicing the sound current, for I have not yet been initiated by the Master. However, let me say this: after I've had the tune-in by the Master, then I will let you know."

They sat in silence for a little while. "Harvey," Florence Kellogg said, breaking the silence. "There is a Tibetan monk visiting in the mountains north of here. I understand that he is practicing this teaching. I heard of him a few weeks ago. I'm told he practices the real art itself. You ought to go see him."

"Where does he stay?"

"In a little mission called La Palma, some twenty miles from here on the coastal highway. His name is Rebazar Tarzs. I really don't know what he is doing here. Now I wish you'd forget this long enough to say the word that you will work for me."

Dodds looked off into the valley at the twinkling lights wondering why there was such a sudden urge in himself to see the Tibetan monk in the mountains. Turning, he nodded to the woman. "I'll let you know right away, Florence."

Lal Ghosh was growing desperately ill over his family affairs. The key of the political campaign hung upon the safety of his daughter and her return to the family fold.

He finally decided that it would be best to write Captain Harvey Dodds about this trouble in his household and that it would be best to send Shyama home since the boy did not apparently want to follow his father's instructions and had not answered the previous letter Ghosh had written him.

Perhaps the boy's presence in the household would bring about the desired change which Bhola Lal Ghosh was seeking. Perhaps his luck would change. And God would smile upon him again and cause the enemy to release Amiya without injury. Then his old life would come back strong and pleasant.

Of course this meant that Shyama would not be able to finish his schooling in America and fulfill his desire of becoming a doctor for the Indian people who needed the services of skilled surgeons more than ever before.

His wife had wept until her body seemed to shrink with the agony of sorrow. She could not possibly have wept any longer because, he knew, that her mind and heart had become dry from the anguish. So, dry-eyed, she went about her household duties each day hoping that her prayers would be answered and the change in their family affairs for the better would come through a miracle in time to save them from the onrushing climax of this awful catastrophe.

So Ghosh sat down on this particular evening and started the letter, dutifully writing his request that the American persuade his son to return home for a short time in order to help with certain problems which could be solved with the boy's presence.

As his pen glided over the paper, the image of the tall, lean, handsome face of Harvey Dodds appeared in his mind, and the emotions of what he was trying to do to this man almost overcame him. As much as he loved Harvey Dodds, there must be some way of luring him back to India. Should he tell the truth and appeal to Dodds' sense of justice? Yet where was justice when it came to bringing Dodds back to

India to swap his life for Amiya's safe return?

He seemed unable to control the pen as it poured out his heart to the foreigner to help save his daughter. He did not seem surprised at what he wrote. A spirit had seized his hand and was putting into expression the great love he had for his daughter.

Quickly he finished the letter and without bothering to read it back sealed the envelope, put an airmail stamp on it and gave it to one of the servants to post at once.

Then he felt sorely troubled in his heart over the contents of the letter in which he had somewhat misrepresented himself and the situation of the Ghosh family, and went into the room where the family altar sat and put himself into deep contemplation for an hour or so, his mind completely upon the Master, beseeching him with prayers to help.

All of a sudden he opened his eyes. Before him stood a tall man cloaked in a white shining light. Fear entered his heart, but he shut it out quickly for it was the Master appearing to him in the subtle body.

The Master looked at him gently. "You called for me, my son?" he said. "No. Do not touch me for it would be dangerous to your physical body.

"The problem which is bothering you, Bhola Lal Ghosh, is you. You have lost your emotional control, and you must overcome this wrong thinking. It is true that, whether we realize it or not, we are directly or indirectly responsible for everything that has

— 156 —

happened to us. Instead of blaming others when things go wrong or feel ourselves to have been mistreated, we should first look for the cause in our own faulty thinking or actions.

"Out of this devastating experience for your family should come the realization which has forever protected the enlightened against troubles by others! No one can hurt you unless you let them hurt you!

"In this painful experience you are holding bitter feelings against the doer of the deed. Is this not true? You are blaming the American for your troubles. This is not true. You brought this problem upon yourself!

"Why give any individual the power to keep on hurting you by becoming emotionally upset and mentally disturbed everytime you think of him?

"Regardless of your seeming justification for such resentment of mistreatment, let go of those destructive feelings. It is impossible for you to apply your mind to other worthwhile activities and objectives as long as it is disturbed by this misfortune.

"Dismiss your feelings, once and for all, with the resolute declaration in consciousness that nobody can hurt you—unless you let them hurt you.

"The great law of the SUGMAD is that you will attract whatever is in your consciousness. Remember, Bhola Lal Ghosh, that it is not the things that happen to us that count. It is how we react emotionally and mentally to what happens. This determines our pain or pleasure and of course our karma in our successive lives."

The shining figure of the great Master gradually faded into nothingness. Slowly Ghosh rose to his feet wondering if he had seen an illusion or was it that he had slept.

Harvey Dodds got up early that morning determined that he would drive up the highway to see the Tibetan ECK Master who Florence Kellogg had spoken about.

He had hardly gotten into his clothes and was preparing to inform Shyama to get dressed to leave when the telephone rang. The call was from Congressman Jack Rhey's office in Washington. He waited for the call to come through wondering why the Congressman wanted him.

"Hello out there, Harvey Dodds!" The Congressman's voice shouted over the wire. "Had a hard time getting you."

There was a slight pause. "I've been all night at a party here in Washington which R. J. Whitfield gave for his friends in order to get another fat government contract. You know R. J.! He's the kind of guy who thinks everybody's got a price and he has the money to pay the price!"

"Must have been some party, Jack!" Dodds said wondering about the call.

"Sure was. But I stayed sober enough to know what was going on. And something concerning you came up, Harvey!"

"Why me? How'd I get in such fast company?"

There was a humming of wires, then the Congressman spoke up. "You know that I'm Chairman of the House unAmerican Activities Committee? R. J.'s been after me to make an investigation on your activities which he thinks are unAmerican. What you been doing, Harvey?"

"Nothing but talk about the religions of India in a public address to a bunch of dames in Four Rivers."

"That's the problem all right. R. J.'s trying to make out like that it goes further than any religious idea. He says it's downright unAmerican for any one to preach that stuff in this country, for according to him, it's the doctrine of the iron curtain countries. He says it's a cult of the unbelievers and it's dangerous to the American way of life!"

"R. J.'s crazy!"

"Crazy or not he's gone bugs on the subject and is chasing me around like a Senator after his secretary to make me get you on the witness stand!"

"Why is he out to get me?" Dodds asked. "Because my father made a bad mistake and killed his wife? That's the start of it, but he thinks I'm trying to get revenge by making Lucia fall in love with me, or some silly nonsense like that. I didn't cause Lucia to leave him—that was of his own doings!"

The Congressman said, "Thought I'd let you know, Harvey. I haven't given in to his

— 159 —

pressure yet. In fact, I had a couple of boys in Four Rivers not long ago checking on you but found nothing. It looks though like he might make me find something on you. If it does happen I'll make it as light as possible on you. Goodbye!"

Dodds hung up wondering if Whitfield would ever stop persecuting him. Then he put in a call for his aunt in Four Rivers who told him that she had heard that Lucia Whitfield had closed her New York apartment and gone back to California. The plant was still out on strike and the people of the city were beginning to create a desperate mood against Whitfield.

He hung up and went to the door to pick up the mail just left. There was a letter from Lal Ghosh. Going inside he fixed a cup of coffee and sat down to read it.

His heart gave a sudden start. The letter was beyond anything he had expected from Ghosh. The man wanted his son to return home to help him with boosting their morale over the problems now facing the family. Beyond that, Gosh appealed to him to personally bring the boy home.

What did Ghosh mean by this? Why, it would put his life in danger to return to India. Amiya was in the hands of the Communists and that was trouble aplenty, but something had to be done to help the Ghosh family.

Shyama came downstairs. Dodds put the letter in his pocket and greeted him casually, then went about getting breakfast. After eating, he decided to face the issue squarely and pulled the letter from his pocket and asked the boy to read it.

When Shyama had finished he handed it back saying, "Yes, I received a letter from him while in New York asking that I return, but it is impossible. I love my family and am sorry to know what has happened but I love you more. There is also the debt of my life to be repaid!"

Dodds said, "That debt has been paid a hundred times to me. It will be hard to part but sooner or later we must do so. If necessary I will do as your father asked and take you back to India myself. It would be no problem for me to give up everything and do that!"

"No," the boy turned pale. "You must never go back. My father didn't mean it."

Curiosity stirred Dodds. "What's wrong, Sammy? Why don't you want me to go back. Is it because you think I'd be in danger?"

"My father will do anything possible to get you back," Shyama said sadly. "He must have that manuscript and yourself to swap for Amiya's freedom. Those are the terms made to him.

"In spite of his great love for you and his sense of honor, he is desperate to get my sister back. I've been instructed to do anything to make you return to India. Once there you would be taken prisoner and shipped back to Red China.

"Please believe me, Harvey. It's only the love for Amiya which turned my father this way!"

Dodds stared at the boy in amazement.

R. J. Whitfield rang for his secretary, then leaned back in his chair. His peace of mind had been disturbed in the past few weeks over the death of Julie Vanners. He was trying to rationalize his actions in this matter but the more he tried the greater the guilt feeling grew in him.

Elsa Spain opened the door and stepped into the office. "Yes, sir!" she said.

"What has become of that piece of paper that Price sent here a few weeks ago?"

"It's locked in your file cabinet. Do you want to see it now?"

"Bring it in, please!"

She returned with a brown envelope. "It's that parchment which is supposed to be a masterpiece. Harvey Dodds and that Indian boy brought it to the states. I checked but found there was no declaration made on it. You may have use for it?"

"This belonged to Dodds and the Hindu?" he said. "Maybe Price had something after all. He kept blabbing away at making money out of it."

"I think so," she said. "I checked with the City Museum and they will look it over if you want to sell."

"You know, Elsa, this might be the way for me to make an extra wad of money in a quick way. The U. S. Oil Corporation is

— 162 —

a cleanup deal for anybody, but I haven't the cash to put into it at this moment. I might get it out of this."

She asked, "You want me to take it over to old Kennedy to see if the Museum would be interested?"

"Not him. He's a bloodsucker. He's rigged me too many times on everything in the art line. Can't you make a direct contact with someone at the Museum?"

"I don't know anything about ancient parchments, R. J., Kennedy does. He can get more cash for it than we could think of, if it's worth anything. He'll know if it's genuine or not."

"Well, all right, but mind you only ten percent for his part and no more. Make it clear to him."

He went out to lunch with some of the office people thinking about Julie Vanners. Maybe he could make it up by giving Rev. Vanners' church a few thousand dollars for a new bell or a glass window. That would ease this off his conscience.

When he returned, Elmo Kennedy, the art dealer, was waiting for him. "I've looked it over, Mr. Whitfield," the man said, "and we can do business provided you pay the right commission."

"Ten percent for you," Whitfield said.

"Twenty-five!"

"I can't make any money that way. You'd probably sell it for ten thousand and that would cut into my take."

The man laughed. "Why man, ten thousand ain't nothing. I can get you twenty-five times that much. I made a call while you were out and the City Museum said that if it's authentic there was a wealthy old geezer who would pay as high as a quarter of a million and give it to the museum."

Whitfield dropped in his chair. "Quarter of a million?" he whispered. "Take your twenty-five percent and be happy!"

He wiped the perspiration off his brow and thought to himself that this was a way to send some money to Rev. Vanners' church as a gift which would help clear himself to God.

CHAPTER 9

Harvey Dodds sent Shyama back to his family, in Srinagar, despite every protest he could think of to keep the boy with him. It almost broke Dodds' heart to do this, yet he was fully aware that it was imperative. Bhola Lal Ghosh needed his son, and the decision caused a break in the friendship between Shyama and Dodds.

The house on the shady lane in the foothills of Hollywood became exceedingly empty to Harvey Dodds. For days he could not get used to the fact that he was alone and was regretful of his decision and action. The presence of the Hindu boy was missed so badly that for a long time Dodds could not even stay in the house.

He spent time in the movies, on long drives through the countryside, and at the beach walking along the sandy shores listening to the beat of the surf, trying to be rid of that guilt feeling that he had made a terrible mistake in sending the boy back to India. What he did might mean the death of Shyama.

Harvey Dodds was sorely afraid. The letter from Bhola Lal Ghosh combined with what Shyama told him about the plot to get himself, Dodds, back into India again had set off a chain of reactions within him. If the Communists wanted him back in India and were working upon Bhola Lal Ghosh to get him there they might become desperate and even murder the Ghosh children.

A feeling of helplessness overcame him whenever he thought of this. What could he do?

Shyama left Los Angeles in frustration and tears. He was in a sullen mood, angry at Harvey Dodds and his father because he believed that his own life was at stake. The letter from Lal Ghosh was so pitiful in its appeal to Dodds for the return of his son that it had broken Dodd's heart. No longer could he entertain the thought of keeping Shyama in America despite the fact that the boy went back without the manuscript, a requisite also included in the demand for Amiya's release.

As for his loneliness, he tried to justify his decision with the fact that the trouble between Bhola Lal Ghosh and the communists would soon run its course and then Shyama would come back to him to finish his education in America. But within his heart he was aware that this wasn't true. He was only making excuses to appease himself.

His own troubles were pestering him for he was conscious of what the telephone call from Congressman Jack Rhey meant. If R. J. Whitfield could force a Congressional investigation of Harvey Dodds' behavior while in the Chinese prison it was logical that the Air Force would be compelled by public opinion instigated by the newspapers to make a complete sweep of its own. There could be little telling what would come out of an action of this kind.

There were plenty of soreheads still left

in the service with whom he had spent time in a Chinese compound, and if any one of them should decide to make charges against him—that he cooperated with the enemy—then there would be a real hard time given him.

He could really be framed into something of which he was entirely innocent.

This seemed to be what R. J. Whitfield was doing. The industrialist was trying to put him in a bad light so the military department would take up the case and make an issue of it.

If R. J. Whitfield did not let up on him and pushed this matter too forcefully, who would know what could happen. Look at what occured to those unfortunate Americans who had returned to this country after imprisonment by the Chinese Reds. Many of them on trial were accused by their fellow prisoners of cooperating with the Reds against the Americans. In most cases it amounted to prejudice and hatred developed between those who had been captured and confined during the Korean War.

Many times there were enough witnesses to make the charge stick and another prison term was given in an American cell. Who knew but what he, Harvey Dodds, might not be put in the same situation if R. J. Whitfield could get enough evidence regardless of what it might be? There might be someone who didn't like him during the prison stay while in Red China and could make it rough for him on a witness stand.

His thoughts returned to Shyama. The

boy had made a scene about returning to India. Smiling, Harvey Dodds laid down on his couch in the living room and smoked. The Hindu lad had adopted enough American habits to make him difficult now; although the training was strong within him the emotion of love between Harvey Dodds and the Indian boy was stronger. He wondered how the communists would take to this idea of sending Shyama home without himself or the manuscript? Would Shyama actually have the courage to get to his home in Srinagar or would he leave the plane somewhere between America and his destination?

Just before the plane took off from the airport he and the boy embraced and wept together; even at the last moment Shyama had to be pushed away and put on the plane. The boy pleaded not to have to leave Harvey Dodds. People watched them, smiling at the scene between the two, but totally unaware that a terrible agony of fear was going on between them. There was nothing that Harvey Dodds could do about it since Shyama was determined to make his demonstration at that time.

Harvey Dodds, however, had consoled the boy and told him that soon he would be coming to India to be with the living ECK Master again. When it would be, he was not quite sure, but to look for him any moment. Shyama protested in fear that he could never come back to India, for his life was not safe there as long as the communists were allowed to openly operate in that country.

Suddenly at the last moment he told Shyama that he was bordering upon the decision to return within a few days to India and give himself up for Amiya's release. That he loved her dearly and if Bhola Lal Ghosh could extract an iron-bound promise out of the Reds on this he would certainly return.

Shyama smiled through her tears. "I'm afraid by that time it will be of little use."

"But I must stay here Shyama until Soul tells me that it is right. When that comes, nothing will stop me."

He drove back to the house thinking about his future. Now was the time for him to get busy again. What to do wasn't certain, but perhaps that job at the Kellogg Clinic wouldn't be so bad after all. It would be a starter for him to begin working again.

He got the woman on the telephone and told her of his decision. It made Florence Kellogg very happy, and she said that it was a decision which he would not regret. She gave him a week to report for work.

R. J. Whitfield swiveled around in his massive chair and lighted a long slim cigar. He was waiting for his daughter to arrive at the office as she had announced by telephone a few minutes before.

Lucia Whitfield entered the office with

a long, confident stride. Her striking poise and compelling beauty instantly put a harmonious feeling into his mood. He was thinking that she was a beautiful girl. It was a fact that every time he saw her his mind was forced to recognize this more and more.

She took a seat in one of the soft, leather chairs near his desk and faced him, looking into his hard, granite face for a long time in a dark, angry gaze. He smiled crookedly, one corner of his mouth pulled up.

"Why did you send for me?" she asked in a forceful tone.

Her voice struck him wrong, setting in motion negative vibrations which made him reply roughly. "I want to get at the bottom of this trouble between us. What's wrong with you?"

"You, father. That's what is wrong with me. What in the name of God has gotten into you? How stubborn can you get?"

He laughed loudly. "What is the trouble now? Still weeping over Harvey Dodds? You should have forgotten him a long time ago!"

"I should have but frankly I didn't, if that is any of your business. Now what is this that you've gone beyond Jack Rhey to the Air Force and asked that they dig up something on Harvey for a charge against his conduct as a prisoner of war. You are going pretty deep aren't you? God's never going to allow you to get away with this!"

He puffed on his cigar and little white balls of smoke flew toward the ceiling.

"Look who's talking about God with that heathen belief in Tibetan religion that's pouring through your mind." He banged the desk with a fist.

"How low can you get? I never thought you'd stoop to this sort of thing. Look at you now. A beautiful woman who could marry just about any man you desire in the country, or in the international set for that matter. But you'd rather play around with a heathen cult and a bunch of ragged tramps who make a practice of fleecing rich men's daughters!"

She said scornfully. "You make a practice of talking God to me whenever there is something in my conduct you don't like! You don't know anything about God. You use God as your tool, so you think. You've tried to buy God with a price just like you do everybody. It's your motto. 'Everything has a price, and I've got the money to pay for it!'

"Even Reverend Vanners is on your payroll. You dumped a lot of money into his church and that makes you a great man with God!

"What did you do for the Reverend when the Board of his Church asked that he be removed from his parish? Nothing, as usual. You had all the use of him that could possibly be, so you quietly sat by and let the poor man talk himself out of his own livelihood and the church!"

"I don't like that kind of talk coming from you, Lucia!" he said low, hard and warningly. "I brought you here to talk over my will! Are you going to listen?"

She ignored him. "And for your information, I'm not marrying anybody that you have got picked out for me. I would marry Harvey Dodds any time, any day in the week if he'd ask me. Now what do you want to see me about?"

He glared at her. "You'd marry that tramp?"

"Yes, I would," she said firmly.

"Then that makes up my mind," he remarked hotly. "I tell you again I asked you here to discuss my will. If you are willing to give me proof that you can give up this nonsense about those oriental philosophies, I'll leave you the entire estate of three million dollars, immediately upon my death, as always planned and which now shows in my will. Otherwise, I will today change my will to distribute a million among my faithful employees, give a half million to the Church in Four Rivers and the rest to my only legal relative, my half-sister, Jane."

She stood up quickly. "So that is what you have been wanting to see me about. I can be bought as you have bought all the others.

"You ought to stop and take a look at yourself, R. J. Whitfield. See how you have used people. You took advantage of poor Reverend Vanners while he was in that terrible state of mind over Julie's death and used him. Now you're throwing him to the wolves. Why don't you will him some of that money? The poor fellow is going to be out in the cold very soon and will be there a long time, and will need some of that cash. What are you going to tell him if he should knock on your door and ask for help?"

She paused and went on. "Why don't you distribute some of that money among your employees instead of a favorite few or give up the profits to that greedy bunch of stockholders. God only knows that they deserve a lot of it from you for all the treatment you've been giving them during the years you've been president!"

Again she said, "Frankly, I don't want any of your money. I'm not for sale today nor any other day!"

"Lucia!" he shouted. "You can't talk to me like that! I'll fix it so that you won't get anything. I can even have your mother's money taken from you!"

She was walking toward the door, then stopped and turned. "I guess you could, father. That is if you tried hard enough. One thing you forget is that it was mother's money that gave you a start in this business. You never loved her. It was because of her inheritance of one million dollars that you married her.

"You loved that and you finally got your hands on most of it, but you didn't get her property which is my source of income. But if you want that, go ahead and take it. I can go to work!"

"My daughter," he said scornfully. "Maybe I have raised a serpent instead of a daughter!"

"Don't say that," she said as her face

paled. "If you want to call names, let me call you one. Murderer! A cheap murderer! You are responsible for Julie Vanners' death! Don't you feel proud about that?"

She slammed the door. Her heels were heard tapping fast on the floor as she ran down the hall. He glared at the glass door, his mind working like a fast locomotive coming down the track.

Suddenly he remembered old Jessie Block, who was a famous baseball player when R. J. was a boy. During the winter Jessie worked on the river as a steamboat engineer. He had foresight and knowledge about R. J.'s future. He had told R. J. that unless he learned to control himself and that awful desire for money that they would get him into serious trouble someday.

Now Jessie's prophecy had come true!

However, it was not the money nor the knowledge that Lucia knew his deepest secret, but his own self-control. He did not like people to flaunt his opinions and desires in his face. His anger flared.

The telephone buzzed. Mrs. Spain said that Congressman Rhey was on the line. The man's voice came through clear, telling Whitfield that the planned attack on Dodds had gone flat. Neither his investigation nor the Air Force could find any evidence to make a charge against the Four Rivers physician.

R. J. Whitfield roared his defiance and hung up trembling with rage. Suddenly a searing pain struck his chest. It came again and again as great fear rose in his mind.

This was curtains for him, he thought. Darkness mercifully cut it off and he fell across the desk unconsciously pulling at the intercom box on his desk.

Elsa Spain heard him and ran into the office. She saw what had happened and called for a doctor, but he arrived too late. R. J. Whitfield was dead.

When Harvey Dodds heard about the news of Whitfield's death he was extremely sorry for Lucia knowing that in spite of her difference with R. J., the girl loved him. Neither did it seem to solve any of the inner turmoil in his heart.

He had made up his mind to see the Tibetan Master visiting in the mountains, north of Los Angeles, before the week was out and he would have to report for work at the clinic.

After getting the directions from Florence Kellogg by telephone he got into his car and drove northward through the range of misty, sunlit hills to the mission where he stopped for a drink of water and asked the direction to Rebazar Tarzs' hut.

He found the shack settled in a lovely little glade on the side of a sloping mountain, at the end of a long lane. He drove up within a few yards of the little hut and stopped the car. Here he got out and looked around but seeing nobody around walked toward the shack.

The place seemed to be, apparently, deserted. No life was anywhere that he could see. However, something about the place attracted Harvey Dodd's attention, but he could not understand what it was at the moment. He stopped approximately ten yards away from the hut feeling very nervous and looking about with anxiety for somebody. All of a sudden he discovered what that strange feeling was in the atmosphere. It was an aura of peace and contentment moving toward him like a wave striking a beach.

Puzzled he stepped back and found that it came in a circle from around the hut. However, it stopped at a certain line. Stepping forward again for a few feet, he found himself again within the circle.

He stood there puzzled, not knowing what to do. This feeling of love seemed to touch his heart, and to make him cry for some unknown reason. Perhaps it was just out of pure joy of finding happiness again. The wave seemed to be coming out of that little shack.

He did not feel like doing the ordinary thing, going up to the door and knocking or calling out to the ECK Master to tell him that he was there. Something stopped him. Instead he sat down in the grass looking at the hut and hoping that the Master would make his appearance right away.

He must have sat there for a good half-hour or more watching the door of the hut before it opened. The feeling of peace was upon him and he could have stayed and rested there throughout eternity. Looking up he saw the strong figure of a man in a maroon robe walking toward him.

At first a feeling of awe swept through him like fire from a dry timber forest. Could it be true? Perhaps it was someone else, not the great Rebazar Tarzs, who was reputed to be over five hundred years old.

Then his heart took a sudden turn for he realized that he was gazing upon the very features of the Master whom he and Shyama had met upon the road to Punjab during his flight from the Reds in India.

The square faced man smiled warmly. "I am Rebazar Tarzs." He spoke perfect English in a deep voice. "I have waited for you a long time!"

"It is you," Harvey Dodds whispered in awe. "We have met before. Who are you? Why are you here?"

Still smiling, the man motioned, beckoning for him to follow. They walked to a shady spot where the grass was thickest, under a cluster of laurels. A small mountain brook rushed down the side of the mountain in a singing, melodious voice. They seated themselves crosslegged upon the ground.

"I cannot answer your questions," Rebazar Tarzs said, his coal black eyes bent upon Dodds. "I am here to tell you something of your future. All that you wish to know will be given in good time. But by the God-man at the proper time, and place!"

He stirred. "You have been searching for a long time for the peace that your heart longs for. You can find that peace only through ECK. The audible life current is the way and method to God. Many seek God through this method and many will succeed. It is not the path that all will find at the same time, but eventually all will come to it. Each to his own channel until the time comes for him here on earth.

"You are seeking the SUGMAD through the art of the audible life stream. You must be given the tests to see if you can succeed. Until you know and succeed, the struggle for God will go on within you throughout your earthly existence. If you are seeking IT through the wrong path then you will be told and your feet be put upon the right path for you."

Harvey Dodds said, "But how will I know about the right path? How am I to know that ECK is the right way to God?"

"You will know by your heart when the Godman desires. Then the heart will recognize through its communication with the Godman. Do not believe the mind for it is always false to you. You must and will be absolutely certain, completely sure in your decision, for once you set upon the path it is like it is stated in Christian teachings, 'When you put your hands upon the plow handle there is no turning back!' The decision is not made by the outer self, but by Soul which knows God for it is a path of God."

"Tell me more about the philosophy of ECK," Dodds said.

"To tell you the way is not so easy. It

cannot be given in words—we just simply run out of words when it comes to defining this. I have never known anyone who can put into words the great music of the universe.

"To be simple about our definition, we say that the audible life stream is the SUGMAD itself vibrating through space. It is the wave of spiritual life going forth from the creator to every living thing in the universe. By that current he makes his creations of all life forms and by it he sustains them. In it they all live and move and have their lives, and by this same stream they will ultimately return to their source of being.

"The higher we go into the upper regions the more beautiful this music becomes. If you pass above the third world into the regions of nothingness, where begins the planes of pure spirit you find that this music is your life, joy and spiritual food. There is not a place in the worlds, any of them, where this heavenly music does not dwell.

"The current, or Word is the only religion, and the only philosophy. Study any philosophy or follow any religion, which does not have this teaching as its central teaching and you will ultimately find your life going off to the side, with obstacles mounting up. It is only the Word that gives all in life as one needs. Without it nothing could live for a single moment or even exist.

"That which the Orientals call prana, a physical energy, is only a manifestation of this life stream, or Word, stepped down to meet material conditions.

"The stream is the fountain of God. It is omnipresent, omnipotent, and omniscient. All energies either latent or dynamic are within it.

"We are all one with this stream. Everything is blessed with the Word. We are like the dewdrops falling into the shining sea for we slip into this sea of light and sound by the essence of our knowledge of the divine Soul."

He paused. "You question the death of the great American capitalist who had to pay his karma through his deeds with mankind. He was the result of over passion and work, the example of those in the western world who find happiness in materiality and personal power."

After a long time Harvey Dodds said "What must I do to find this path of knowledge and love?"

"I can tell you this," the deep voice of the ECK Master lifted above the rushing sounds of the brook. "The lesson of your life can only be found through love. Then all will be given through the living ECK Master. When you have the proper inner preparation then you will be taken into the Godman's fold.

"Now look here. I tell you that the lesson can be learned only through sacrifice. The decision, however, lies only within you to go to the Godman and learn what this lesson might be. The sooner you do, the quicker Soul will start its journey to the true home.

"Again I say, go back to India and see what the Master will say to you!"

Harvey Dodds looked at the Tibetan with amazement. "But I cannot go back to India. My life is in danger there. I will be sent back to the prison in Red China."

The Tibetan smiled gently. "You must believe in the Master. Go and see what he wants with you!"

Harvey Dodds drove back to the city again filled with tormenting doubts. If the path was so hard to follow why should he try it? Why was this mysterious Master always showing up in his life? He was sure that Rebazar Tarzs was the same one whom he and Shyama had met on the road through the Punjab.

Could he take a chance on getting back into India without the communists knowing it. This thought crossed his mind several times. Just how the Master had the answers to his problems of life was yet to be learned but in that brief hour's ride back to the house Harvey Dodds had made up his mind to go to India and see the Swarachakraji. The thought frightened him, but he knew that any danger which was risked was minute in comparison to that great inner urge driving him to the very jaws of death.

He got home and without waiting began to pack his things, scarcely eating when the cook called him to dinner. He told her that

— 181 —

he was closing the house and that she could have a month's salary to look for another job.

The next movement was to see about the air schedules to India and check his passport. He packed a great number of things and called Florence and told her that he was coming by.

Then he drove downtown to a telegraph office and sent a wire to the Master saying that he would be in India within a week. Following this he made reservations for air travel to India, and then went to the passport office to make application for leaving the country.

It was getting late in the afternoon so he went back to the parking lot for the car and drove up to Florence Kellogg's house on the hill overlooking the city.

She was alone. So Dodds started in without hesitation saying it was impossible for him to take her job as the Tibetan had told him to go back to India to see the Master. She registered disappointment but was sympathetic in her understanding and told him that it was well for she could make contact with another surgeon who wanted to come into her clinic. However, if he got back from India within the next few months she could try to fit him into a place on the staff.

A cab drove up outside and someone came to the door. The woman went to the door and opened it. To the surprise of all, including Dodds, Lucia Whitfield walked into the room.

She stopped quickly and looked at Dodds. "You?" she exclaimed. "I should have telephoned first. I've been in town a few days and thought about running out to see you. The clinic told me you were home for the evening."

She went up to Dodds and shook hands. "Hello, Harv," she said with a deep light glowing in her eyes.

"Hello, Lucia," he said feeling stuffy with speaking such words.

They talked for a few minutes, then Florence Kellogg got up and said, "I'll go put on a pot of coffee and get some cake for you."

Dodds sensed the woman knew that he and Lucia wanted to be alone for a few minutes and was grateful.

Lucia said "Thanks for that nice letter about father's death."

"It was the least I could do," he said awkwardly looking at his hands and thinking of the day in New York when she kissed him.

"I know what you are thinking, Harvey," she said. "But I didn't come out here after you. I had to for a reason. Father had a piece of property in Santa Monica and I'm here to make a deal with a realty company who wants it for commercial property."

"I understand, but there is nothing that can be done about the way I feel. You know that R. J. gave me such a bad time that I naturally feel you're a part of him."

She wiped her eyes. "Let's leave R. J. out of this. He can't hurt you anymore!"

"He was a great man in his way!"

She said, "It wouldn't have been so bad except that I feel that I was a part of the cause of his last heart attack. He has had them for years but wouldn't pay any attention to them. That was R. J. for you. He preached the philosophy of the self-made man. Always thought that was the end of living. God didn't even exist in his mind. God was a toy and a plaything for the masses of people to be hypnotized by, for those like himself to have control over. You'd thought he invented God!

"The only thing that R. J. loved was money. He tolerated me but was always puzzled why I could never come under his control. He really drove himself to death, but I could have been a little kinder and loving toward him although he would never have controlled me."

Harvey Dodds said, "I've had a deep concern about you since hearing the news about his death. But knowing you, I thought there would be every reason that you would get over his death quickly. You inherited the whole estate, didn't you?"

She nodded. "That was what killed him. He had called me to the office to discuss changing it, if I didn't give up my search for God.

"I'm having the attorney get a job for Reverend Vanners somewhere in the corporation. Since he got kicked out of his church the poor fellow has almost starved to death. I've persuaded him to become a consultant for our plants in the midwest.

"I am also trying to get the Gatewood directors to cut down on the profits sharing plan with its stockholders and divide the melon each year with the employees and give the old timers some good stock.

"And I am trying to get money for the employees at the Four Rivers plant, and a hospital of some sort built there in memory of Julie Vanners." She stopped and took a deep breath.

"You are going to be shocked, Harvey, but I know that R. J. was the responsible person for Julie's death. He admitted it to me the last time I was in Four Rivers!"

He sat up quickly, staring at the girl. Amazed, he shook his head. "Things are happening too fast for me, Lucia," he murmured. "What about the manuscript? Did you ever find it?"

"Not yet. But I am willing to try and help the Ghosh family on that. I will try to raise money for payment of the scroll and an agreement if that parchment is found my money will be returned from out of the sale."

"That's more than fair," Dodds said.

"I don't know what my future will be, Harvey. But frankly, I'd like to return to India to see the Master and find out what this money can do for his organization. If he wants it all, then he can have it. All I need is enough to live comfortably on for the rest of my life. What mother left will do that easily enough."

Dodds said slowly, "I'm leaving next week for India to go back to the Master, but do not tell anyone. My life is in danger while there."

He told her of his visit with the Tibetan monk. She became excited and spoke up telling him about the same being who appeared in the lobby of the hotel in New Delhi and gave the message about Dodds' escape from the communist prison and being at the ashram.

"I wondered who it could be?" she concluded.

Florence Kellogg came into the room at that moment with a tray of coffee cups and a huge pot. "I see that you two have gotten together again," she said cheerfully.

Harvey nodded with his eyes on the girl. He saw her now with new understanding.

CHAPTER 10

Harvey Dodds reached Bombay after two days of flying across the far reaches of the Pacific by airplane. When he stepped from the plane the very atmosphere seemed to be so much different from that which he had felt before.

There was a familiarity of feeling about this broad, old land where millions of feet trod the highways that led to the great shrines of the Indian gods in the heights of old mountains to the north of this vast land.

The broad blue sky was deeper in its color than he had ever seen a morning sky. The pennants around the field fluttered in the wind. This was India. This was his India. Its great spiritual forces seemed to sweep down and lift Soul completely out of his body.

He checked his baggage in a locker in the airport building where great crowds of people mingled through corridors impatiently awaiting their planes to take off for some distant parts of the world.

He went into a telephone booth, at one end of the building, and put in a call for Shyama, at Srinagar. While awaiting the call to be put through he thought of this life into which he had been unexpectedly thrust by his decision to return to see the Living ECK Master. There had been no answer to his wire so he wondered if the Godman wanted to see him.

After a while the phone rang and he

talked with the operator. She said the connection between Bombay and Srinagar seemed to be having difficulty. He might have to wait four hours before getting through for there had been a storm which had torn down the wires.

He got his baggage and left the airport for a hotel, planning to take a night plane for Srinagar. Later he was told that all air flights for the north had been cancelled because of the storm. He then made reservations by train for the following morning.

Dodds washed up in the hotel room and laid out some light clothes for wearing, then lay down in bed to sleep for a couple hours. His thoughts turned to the Master whose wisdom he had remembered, especially that morning in the Ashram when the sunlight was lying across the mountains and fields.

"If you put the power of Soul into every act, however small, or commonplace, you will have revealed to all who, and what you really are!

"The only way to develop a perception of truth in large things is to trust absolutely to your perception of truth in small things!"

Turning over on the pillow he went to sleep only to awaken later and find the gold of the day had passed and a soft velvet twilight had set in with a short, quick shade of darkness. His mood had changed to a more subtle pattern.

He arose from the bed, washed the sleep out of his eyes and put on the clothes which had been laid out, then went down to the dining room where there was a good English menu and ate heartily. Afterwards he tried another call for Shyama to discover that the lines between Bombay and Srinagar were still down.

Then he walked along the streets window shopping. Strolling slowly down the street he had a queer, vague thought of Soul seeking a release to the satisfaction of Itself. Why had he come six thousand miles to find relief from this strife within himself? Why did Soul make him give up everything in his native land to seek out the unknown, when it meant the greatest personal danger? It was like hearing the call of the wild—the roar of the old lion on the hill which awakens the leonine nature in the lion cub which had been reared among the sheep. The call of the wild duck which bid the domesticated wild bird to use its wings and forsake its barnyard environment. He had heard the deep calling to the depths of Soul. He felt within the stirring of that awakening which had been aroused from its dreamstate. What was he going to do about it?

Suddenly there came an alarm within him, a feeling that made him turn to see a man walking toward him in the half-light of the windows. When the man saw that he was being watched, he turned quickly to act interested in something in a shop's window.

Dodds knew instantly that the man was following him. For what reason could it be? Of course the man was shadowing him. Perhaps to rob him. The Communists could not have known that he was in India.

It flashed into his mind that he had seen that ugly face somewhere before. It was an evil face that would stick in his mind. Turning fully, he got a complete glimpse of the man's countenance, but the shadower saw what was happening and tried to dodge back into the shadows. In that minute Dodds saw all that he needed to know.

He recognized the man. That was one of Nath Dwark's men who had tried to capture him that day at the camp of the Kazakhs where Amiya came into his tent to warn him.

The surprise was so startling that he could only stand staring at the shadows where the man had disappeared. His mouth gaped in a frozen position. Why would Rosha be following him in Bombay, almost immediately upon his arrival in India? He had not been in the country over five hours, and he had not told anybody that he was coming to India, not even Shyama.

Yes, he had! He had told Lucia Whitfield that evening in Florence Kellogg's home. But that was impossible. He shrugged off the thoughts.

Amiya was growing more discouraged daily. The wait for her release grew into days, into weeks and now into months. She thought it impossible to ever see her family again. Nath Dwark visited often bringing a new delicacy for her palate or a word about her family. She always appreciated his visits though they were not too often for Ling suspected Dwark's emotional ties with Amiya. There was little for her to do. She was far matured for her age to try any intelligent discussions with the men for they were simple hill people hired to work for the Communists. Most of them were extremely loyal to Nath Dwark but the Red agent, Ling, had bought them with gold and they were switching loyalties.

Ling visited her twice and tried to talk about the glories of communism but did not succeed in getting far. She had a sharp mind and countered him on every point. Soon he grew angry at his inability to cope with this tiny, highly intelligent woman and gave up, leaving the hut muttering to himself while puffing fiercely on his cigar.

This evening Nath Dwark rode into camp and came to her prison hut where she was sitting outside watching the twilight. The big man looked at her tenderly as he seated himself on the ground nearby. She matched his gaze wondering if it was possible that she was in love with this gigantic bandit chieftain.

"You seem very worried this evening, Nath Dwark," she said slowly, feeling that she was basking in the light of his love. "Is there bad news again? What could be as bad as that you've brought me in the past?"

"There is something serious," Dwark muttered. "I must tell you although it may distress you."

"I have gone far past being distressed. Tell me!"

He fumbled with his Fez briefly. "Your brother is back in India," he said slowly. "He arrived two weeks ago today. I didn't know anything about it until two days ago. He came unexpectedly!"

Joy danced through her heart. Shyama had come home. This was wonderful for it would give her father and mother great joy to have him there again. She smiled through her tears.

He shook his great head. "It is not good news, my dear one. Shyama did not bring the parchment back with him. Neither did the American come. You are still a prisoner!"

She sat silently looking at her hands.

"Your brother might as well stayed in America. His life would not have been in the danger it is now. He hasn't yet grasped the understanding of your predicament and seems very indifferent to the problem. His behavior is far from pleasing. He treats the girls in a frivolous manner so much different than during the old days when he was a virtuous lad of many lovable qualities."

She frowned with pain.

"Your mother scolds him for the way he is acting. But I am told that it has made little impression upon the boy, instead he seems to have grown very sullen toward everybody in the household. I wonder if he could be lonely for the American?"

"What can I do, Nath?" she murmured tearfully. "If they take Shyama and bring him here, then I will certainly die. And it would kill my parents!"

He said gruffly, "Why don't you write the American and get him back? Then Ling will be satisfied with making an even trade with you."

"That isn't fair, Nath. The American cannot be tricked like that!"

"Tell him everything and appeal to him to come to help. Is that trickery?"

"No. It is the only way I will do it. When can you pick up my letter?"

"This evening at eight. Take your regular walk past the guard up the path to the forked tree, turn and start back. There is a clump of brush on your right as you return to the cabin. I will be there waiting to take your letter. Just drop it on the ground!"

She looked into his face. "I will not forget this if we get out alive!"

"If this plan fails I will try to carry you off by force!"

He left her. She went into the hut and wrote the letter to Harvey Dodds, explaining all and asked that he come to India to help her. Before ending she felt compelled to express a strong admiration for him.

Then she went for the walk to meet Dwark. The sentry hardly noticed her pass. The mountains were a rugged landscape against the great world, snows gleaming in the light of a great rising moon. The trees stood straight and tall in the forest and her thoughts were upon the Master.

The man standing at the bend of the road was dressed in a maroon robe, his eyes were like burning coals. He said in a deep voice, "I have a message for you, Amiya Ghosh!"

She stopped quickly. Sudden intuition flashed into her mind. "Are you the Master, Rebazar Tarzs?" she said, hopes arising.

He nodded briefly. "There is little need to give that letter in your pocket to Nath Dwark. Your plan will not work for the tall American is in India. He will soon be at your parents' home. And your father must not betray him to the Communists but send him on to the Master. And he must take your brother with him."

"How can I tell my father?" she asked softly.

"Ask Nath Dwark to take the message to your father. Tell him that it is the will of God."

The Master strode off into the moonlight and disappeared in the forest.

She moved quickly toward the clump of brush to tell Nath Dwark the news.

Nath Dwark reached home late that night wondering at the news which the girl had given him. He was sitting in his bedroom wondering at the girl for it seemed that her mind had snapped under the strain. ECK Masters telling her that the American was in India. Bah! What a story! He was crying in his heart over her condition.

One of the servants rapped on the door and told him that Rosha, who was acting as a Bombay agent, was waiting outside to see him.

Dwark was surprised, but went out to see the man. No doubt the scoundrel was there to get money. Rosha was standing by the door in the living room. Dwark said roughly, "You've come for money. I should cut your throat!"

"No!" Rosha cried. "I'm not here for money. I had to come for there was no way of sending you a message. The storm blew down the telephone poles!"

"What is so important that you left your post in Bombay to risk me cutting your throat?"

Rosha cried, "The American is here. I saw him step off the plane in Bombay!"

"What's this?" Dwark seized the man by his blouse.

"The American, Dodds, has returned. I followed him in Bombay. I determined his identification!"

"You're a fool. The American wouldn't come back!"

"But it's true! It's the same man! I can prove it. Here! I stole some of his papers. There is his name on them. What would I be doing with his papers if he isn't in India?"

Dwark took the papers and examined them. Sure enough, they were letters addressed to Harvey Dodds and the date on them was recent. Rosha had found something of great importance to him.

This could be trickery. Of course it was a trick. Only a trap to catch him in something and Rosha was in the hire of the Indian Secret Police. He half-raised his fist, then dropped it. Suppose that Rosha was telling the truth. Didn't Amiya say the ECK Master told her the same thing?

But suppose that Dodds was cooperating with the Indian police to trap Dwark and his Red agents. It was possible. His hesitation gave him doubt. He said quietly, "You go back and watch the American. Let me know his movements. I will fix it so he will never return to America!"

Rosha said tremblingly, "I had to hire somebody to watch for me while I came here. He has to be paid."

"How much?"

"Twenty rupees!"

"You're a thief!" Dwark cried roughly. "I could have hired ten men for that amount. Tell me how much profit are you going to make on this?"

"None. The thief robbed me. He knew how important this work was so he took advantage of my generosity!"

"Take it." Dwark threw the money to the man. "But be sure to earn it. If you don't, I'll kill you. Hear me?"

He went back into his bedroom wondering if he should prepare to rescue Amiya.

By now, Harvey Dodds was confident that the man who had been shadowing him was the follower of the Red agent Nath Dwark, who was known as Rosha. He became apprehensive of his decision to have returned to India. Perhaps he could catch the plane back to America that night. Fear began to creep into his heart.

When he returned to the hotel that evening to pick up his baggage he discovered that somebody had rifled his luggage and stolen some letters. They were unimportant letters and it made him wonder why they were the only things taken. They were just personal notes from friends that he desired to keep in contact with.

This was proof that something was wrong. How had they discovered his return to India so soon? Was it by coincidence as he stepped off the plane? Or was it that somebody in America, maybe Lucia, had tipped off the Indian Reds? Who in America besides the passport office, the airlines and Lucia knew anything about this trip?

Every time he looked out the window of the hotel there was a shadow standing near the lamp post, watching. Cold shivers raced down his spine. Just how was he to get out of that hotel without them knowing that he was gone? Looking at his watch, he saw there was only an hour left before train time.

Cutting off the light he stood in the darkness watching the man in the street. The shadow saw that the light was out and moved away from the lamp post, threw away his cigarette, pulled his hat low over his face and walked toward the hotel entrance.

Harvey Dodds picked up his luggage and left the room. He caught the elevator down to the lobby, paid his bill and purposely told the cashier that he was going to Calcutta that evening, hoping the shadower would hear and pass the word along. No doubt by now Dwark was in Bombay.

Going outside he caught a cab for the station but watched through the rear window to see if anyone was following. Only once did he see a car which could have been that of somebody following. He got to the station and went inside to pick up his railroad tickets to Calcutta, knowing that he would get off at Hyderabad and catch a plane to Srinagar to find Shyama. For some reason he knew the boy was in danger and perhaps he could help.

He went to the gate, crossed the rail platform to the sleeping car where his compartment was and got ready for bed. He lay down with a revolver under his pillow, waiting to see what would happen. Apparently nothing came so he dropped off to sleep, awakening only once that night when the train pulled out of a station.

The next morning he dressed quickly, put

his luggage together and hopped off the train at Hyderabad. Nobody looked suspicious to him as he went out to a cab and rode to the airport. He was in luck for a plane was taking off for Srinagar within the hour. He went into the dining room to eat and there his heart took a tumble. The shadower was sitting at the counter eating breakfast.

Without giving any attention to the man, Dodds took a table in one corner and ordered. At this point he didn't care what happened to himself.

Strangely, the man did not get on the plane. But Dodds knew the answer, or thought he did. He had wired ahead about the movements which the American was making. Nath Dwark would be waiting for him at the airport in Srinagar. That was simple. He would get off at the first stop and take a train into the city. This he did and completely missed seeing anyone who looked dangerous to him.

He arrived at the Ghosh household at seven in the evening. The place looked about the same as it had since that day Amiya had brought him there from the camp of the Kazakhs to that broad, flat-topped white residence. Chickens clucked about the yard and a pond down in a far corner was filled with honking geese.

Twilight had begun to drop over the earth. A pattern of powdered rice on the threshold from the early morning ritual was still there. It was the Hindu worship of the spirits that guarded the entrance of the home.

This was the evening hour, the hour of union between darkness and light, the hour when the Hindu's said that Soul most easily found Itself one with the infinite Soul. They called it the cowdust hour because this was the time the cows returned to their homes and blessed the one who took the dust off their feet with reverence.

The women of the house had gone to the roof-tops for meditation. Bells in temples and homes were calling men to evening worship. Harvey Dodds could hear the ancient prayer going on around him, as he stood there watching the beautiful sight of darkness creeping in along the willow trees.

"Harvey." A voice which he had heard many times in the last few months. "Is that you? You're not a spirit are you? Let me touch you!"

The boy was hugging him tightly. "It is you again, Harvey," he whispered. "You've come for me. Thank God!"

"I'm here Sammy. I've come back to India. I never want to be separated from you again. You're in danger and I had to come."

The boy pulled back with tears in his eyes. "Do I act like a child? I can't help it!"

Others discovered him and poured out of the house to greet him. Bhola Lal Ghosh came toward him beaming, with his hands out in greeting.

They went into the library where Harvey Dodds sat in one of the leather chairs and lighted a cigarette. He told them about the events in America that led up to his return to India, then about the shadower in Bombay and Hyderabad whom he believed to be one of Dwark's agents. Turning to Ghosh he told of his desire to return to see the Living ECK Master and why he had come to Shyama. He believed that Shyama was in danger.

Ghosh repeated his story of Amiya's abduction and the situation in his household. He was desperate to get Dodds to India again to solve his problem and asked the real reason why the American was back.

Dodds looked at Shyama who seemed to read his mind and nodded. Then he told about the ECK Master whom they had met on the road and of his experience in the mountains of California."

Bhola Lal Ghosh smiled. "He was Rebazar Tarzs who is the greatest ECK Master in this whole world. You are fortunate for he is guiding your life."

"If this is true, why does he want to keep his hand in my affairs?" Dodds asked.

"He may have a great mission for you," the householder said seriously for the first time in weeks showing interest in anything. "One can never tell what he is doing."

"I am very curious about this Viswapati. Who is he and what does he do in this world?"

"Ah, there is a great mystery, Captain Dodds. Viswapati is a person or being of great mystery. He is a great ECK Master. Many legends say that he is our living Master in another form, or vice versa — but let us not talk about it now."

Dodds said, "Why?"

"There is a matter of personal concern,"

said Ghosh. "Now since you are here of your own free will, then I know that it is the Will of God to help get my daughter back. For that reason I will not help Dwark in his plan to recapture you. You want to get to the ashram right away?"

Dodds nodded. "It is dangerous for me to stay here. Dwark might make new threats against your family and involve Sammy. Can I take the lad with me to the ashram?"

"Of course. It will be safer for him there. But I warn you that unless we have some results in getting my daughter back within a few days your presence will be reported to the Communist secret agents here to swap you for release!

"I will let nothing stand in my way to get her back again!"

CHAPTER 11

Lucia Whitfield returned to New York City from Los Angeles in a very discouraged mood. She was certain that any relationship between herself and Harvey Dodds was at an end. Nothing that either could possibly do would ever be able to put back together that old feeling that they both once possessed.

She was aware that by now Harvey Dodds was on his way across the wide Pacific to India. That very soon he would be sitting on the verandah of the cottage in the ashram, at Kumur, drinking in the wisdom of the great ECK Master, Swarachakraji. How she envied him and wished that she had the opportunity to leave the states immediately for India. Only the business of settling some of the affairs of her father's estate with the attorneys kept her in New York City.

Already the relatives of the family, even those who were so remote that there was only the slightest speaking terms between them, had begun to clamor at her door for claims on the great estate left by R. J. Whitfield. This only served to make her more disgusted with the world of people of this kind.

She had now come to the decision that the spiritual life was not possible for her and with the relatives wanting to take to court their claims for the breaking of R. J's will by trying to prove that Lucia was not competent because of her interest in the strange eastern religion, she was thinking it was best to marry one of the eligible young bachelors who was serving as a vice president in the corporation.

She should settle down as R. J. had begged her for years to do and raise a family.

Three brilliant young executives had been eyeing her for a long time, and it would only be a matter of picking out the one most suited to her temperament and saying yes. Still she just couldn't get interested.

She telephoned her attorney that morning and asked. "How long do you think it will take you to get things in order?"

"That depends upon what you mean by things in order?" the attorney replied.

"I might want to leave the country for several months. In fact, if I should go, it's impossible to say how long I would be gone. If it is necessary that I would have to stay here, please let me know right away. Or should I be overseas and you would need me here fast, would it be possible to contact me at once?"

"Where are you going? On a safari through the Congo?" he asked.

She laughed. "No, I'm going to India, if possible. May be there for months. I really do not know but if it is not possible for me to leave at this time, the idea of the trip can be given up at once!"

"I do not see why you couldn't go, Miss Whitfield. If somebody wants to take the case to court to break the will it would be months before the machinery of the law could get into action.

"With an estate such as this one there

would be a lot of legal paper work to be done. However, I can fully assure you that unless your father made another will, at an earlier date, which has not yet shown up, there is nothing to prevent you from receiving the entire estate. His will, as filed in the state of New York, clearly states that you are the sole heir to his property."

She said, "I will authorize you to establish a trust fund for my Aunt Jane Whitfield at Four Rivers to provide an income to her for the rest of her life. D. J. was providing her with the usual comforts, but I want to double the amount so that it will take care of any extra expenses that she might have. Will you make those provisions and send the papers over to me for my signature?"

"Yes, I will do it at once," he replied. "I will draw up the necessary papers for your signature. However, there is another complication which has arisen. A check came to the office this morning for R. J. Whitfield. Quite a tidy sum of money. It amounts to a quarter of a million dollars."

"What?" she exclaimed. "Where did it come from?"

"From the City Museum. It is in payment for an ancient scroll that your father sold them a few days ago. I don't know what to do with it."

Astonishment struck her in hard waves numbing her brain so thought would not come. What she had heard was true. R. J. did actually steal that manuscript from Shyama and sold it to the City Museum.

Goodness gracious but this put her in a very bad situation. What could she do about it? Frankly, there was nothing except to pay that money to the Ghosh family. She made that decision in a moment. She now had to go to India and explain to Shyama's people what had happened and give them the check.

She said quickly, "I've made up my mind. You hold that check for me until I can get down to the office. Don't give me any argument. Soon as my passport is ready I will leave for India by air. Here is my address there so if you need me either call by international telephone or send a cablegram." She reached for a pad on her desk and read off the address and telephone numbers of both the Ghosh household in Srinagar and the ashram at Kumur. "Of course you can always get me through the American Ambassador at New Delhi!"

"I don't know what to say, Miss Whitfield. But you will explain when you get here at the office? Can you see me this afternoon? I would like to get the matter of this check straightened out. Two hundred and fifty thousand dollars is a lot of money to be left lying around!"

She said, "Just one thing more. Suppose that I would want to give away my estate or part of it? Is that possible under the present status?"

"Why yes. I can see no reason why you cannot give away every penny of it, should you desire to do so. Are you thinking about that?"

"Just thinking. No decision. Goodbye I will see you this afternoon at three."

She began packing her clothes and making ready to close her New York apartment. However, friends got the word by grapevine that she was leaving for India again, and started dropping in to give their advice against the trip. Most of them were girl friends and they were all interested in the fact that she was in the danger of losing a prospective husband among the corporation's young executives. All the prospects would be married and settled down by the time she got back. And was it true she was going to give away all that money her father had left?

Lucia was impatient. This chatter was wearing her down.

Firmly, but politely, she told each that if she missed marriage in America at this particular time, there would be plenty of other men in the firm, and if not there, others in the world who wouldn't let her three million dollars inheritance go to waste. Somebody would always be around and pick up what they could of her money.

It made her visitors uncomfortable and very unhappy, but nevertheless they left satisfied that Lucia was going mad. To chase a miracle monger half-way around the world was something they couldn't understand and told her so. Lucia got fed up with this voluntary advice and locked her apartment and went to a hotel where none of her friends could find her.

This was the way she stayed until her passport came through and then she got tickets for India on one of the overseas flights. It would take three days to get some domestic Indian airline for Srinagar to meet Harvey Dodds and the Ghosh family and turn the check over to Shyama. From there she would go directly to the ashram at Kumur.

She wasn't at all certain how Bhola Lal Ghosh would take this story. But she was willing to amend the situation by offering him the original check as payment on the debt.

The trip across the ocean and over Europe down through Western Asia was uneventful. She arrived in Bombay a few days later and flew to Srinagar to hear that Harvey Dodds and Shyama had left for the Ashram at Kumur. She was left there alone to explain the mystery of the missing manuscript, and offer Bhola Lal Ghosh the check made out in her father's name.

Her heart wasn't in the task.

Bhola Lal Ghosh puzzled over his visitor's return to his home, all the way from America, to offer him a large sum of money for the lost manuscript.

He had a mixture of feelings, swayed by delight with the offer of an unusually large sum, for it would purchase the freedom of his daughter. On the other hand, he was pestered with doubt and discouragement because the Reds had demanded the actual scroll. What would they do?

Perhaps now was the time for him to see his old enemy, Nath Dwark and talk over the proposed plan for releasing Amiya and paying the ransom with good rupees. Dwark had been pretty decent during the whole situation and now it was time to test the bandit chief's real good will. However, he wasn't sure just how Dwark would receive him now.

Since the return of the American, Harvey Dodds, to his house and departure for Kumur to the Master's Ashram with his son, Bhola Lal Ghosh had a feeling of confidence surge back into himself. He was feeling much better now and was going fairly regularly to his offices to conduct the daily routine with his usual high efficiency as of old. His wife looked upon him again with a more pleased expression in her eyes.

He went out into the yard this morning and found her making a pattern of powdered rice on the threshold as a part of the early morning rituals for the worship of the spirits that guarded the entrance to their home.

He waited until she had finished and gone out to throw grain to the crows and crumbs to the insects and feed a holy beggar at the door step. After this came breakfast which she served him first, fasting until after he had eaten. He watched her finish her breakfast then spoke to her about the problem on his mind.

"You are right, my husband," she spoke in a sing-song voice. "The woman has somewhat created a problem by bringing the money and not the scroll of the ancient one. How will Chung Ling take this? It is my opinion that he will like the money and might take it, but hold our daughter longer for further use!"

Ghosh replied, "The American woman, Miss Whitfield, is a splendid person who believes in the SUGMAD. She has done what she believes is right, and I agree with her. However, we did send the manuscript to America, by our son, to be sold. We wanted money, a large sum of it, for the purpose of helping ourselves, but things have changed, my wife. We are left with nothing at all, not even our daughter, for the money means nothing without her in our household again, safe and well. Perhaps we should not even tell the Red agent Chung Ling that we have received the money for the scroll."

"Why not, my husband?" she cried urgently. "Would you let your daughter die in that monster's hands? She has probably been sorely mistreated so badly now that it will take months for her to recover—and perhaps she will not recover at all!"

"I will go immediately to Dwark and ask for contact with Chung Ling," he replied, quickly trying to escape her outburst.

After breakfast Bhola Lal Ghosh set out on his journey to Dwark's office with a reluctant feeling in his heart. He was not sure that this was the right thing to do. For if Chung Ling was going to be unfair again, as in the case of that agreement, then he was wasting his time and the money.

But what else did he have to offer?

He arrived at the office and was greeted by Nath Dwark who took him into a narrow cubicle and seated him before the desk, then gave him a cup of wine. Lal Ghosh wondered at this treatment, which was so much unlike his old enemy.

"This is an unexpected visit, Lal Ghosh," the big, hawk-nosed man said. "What has brought you to my office so early in the day? Are you planning something that will affect me in the coming election? If so, let me tell you that little do I care except that Chung Ling will not like it."

Lal Ghosh shook his head. "I've come to talk with you on a secret matter, Dwark. This is something that is between you and myself, concerning the return of my daughter to my home. Your advice is needed!"

"Can you trust me, Lal Ghosh? You know that I am your enemy, but suspect that you are taking advantage of my love for your daughter. Is that not true?"

"That is true, Dwark," Ghosh added.

"Then tell me what is on your mind."

Ghosh told him about the money received for the manuscript. "I don't know what to do, Nath Dwark. If I offer the money to Chung Ling, then all may be wasted for he might take the money but hold Amiya longer for further advantages. I know not what they could be but there is nothing that he can think of which isn't possible."

Dwark tapped the desk with his fingers for a long time and then said, "I do not know what is the correct answer, Bhola Lal Ghosh, but I believe that it is best to offer him the money since the scroll is no longer in your hands. Perhaps it is best to send him a message stating this data but offering only a certain sum far less than the payment of the scroll. If he agrees to exchange Amiya for the money, make him deliver the girl first before passing over the money!"

"That is an excellent idea, Nath Dwark," Ghosh said slowly while studying over the plan in his mind. "Would you act as my messenger to Chung Ling?"

Dwark's great countenance changed rapidly to doubt, then back to its original composure. Finally he said, "Yes, I will do the job for you provided that you enter into an agreement with me, Bhola Lal Ghosh. Are you willing to look forward to an agreement with me again?"

"I don't know why not, Dwark. You have been very decent about this matter of mine. In fact, I didn't ever expect that you would take the attitude toward me that you have in this time of my trial in life. What is it that you want of me this time?"

Dwark hesitated, "Well, it's like this, Bhola Lal Ghosh." He scratched his cheek. "We've been enemies for a good number of years, in some ways more than we can count. If I win the election this year it will be at your expense, but that's something which I do not relish, even though six months ago it would have made me extremely happy. What I ask of you is this. If Amiya is returned to you in safety, and if she is willing, may I have the honor of calling upon her and asking for her hand in marriage?"

Lal Ghosh jumped to his feet as the words struck him with a giant force. "Why?" he exclaimed with perspiration running down his cheeks. "Why, I don't know, Nath Dwark. But let's leave that to Amiya. She must make that decision herself!"

Dwark learned early that day, after Lal Ghosh's visit, that Harvey Dodds had arrived in Srinagar and left again with Shyama for the ashram at Kumur. Everything was happening so quickly that he hardly had time to think about any of it.

This intelligence had caught him by surprise but the offer that Bhola Lal Ghosh had made to Chung Ling about payment of money for Amiya's release was stronger in his mind than anything else. He raged at his failure to grasp the significance of what was happening. He was certain that his mission to see Ling would be a failure for Ghosh.

He knew that Rosha had carefully watched the American leave Bombay, followed him to where he got off the train enroute to Calcutta and took a plane for Srinagar. The only trouble was that nobody, even himself, remembered to instruct the men to be on the lookout for the American. As a result nobody witnessed his arrival in Srinagar.

Dwark was more confused now that the daughter of the late American capitalist, Miss Lucia Whitfield, had arrived in the city and was trying to dicker with Bhola Lal Ghosh over the payment of the scroll of Fubbi Quantz. His brain whirled around like the notes of music coming out of a woodwind.

He was quite fearful, however, that Chung Ling would accept the money and neglect Amiya's safety. The Red Secret Agent was really not a man of his word.

Dwark decided upon one course of action. That he would present Bhola Lal Ghosh's request to Ling but if the Red chief showed any signs of treachery, it meant he had to kill Ling. Amiya's life was at stake and that was more precious than his own.

He checked the load in his revolvers, thrust them into the gay cummerbund around his thick waist and loosened the dagger in his sheath. Then he went out to his stable and saddled the great, iron-gray stallion. He rode through the late evening into the hills, up the slopes to the camp where Ling was engaged in a game of chess with some of his men.

First, however, Dwark went to the cabin where Amiya was prisoner to find her walking the path for her daily exercise. He waved the guard aside and joined her.

"Your Master was right," he spoke in a

low cautious voice, then told her that the American was at the Ashram with her brother. "I saw your father today. He asked that I convey a message to Chung Ling. He is willing to pay a large sum of money for your release."

"A large sum of money!" she exclaimed "But where in the world would he get any large sum of money? How much does he propose?"

"One hundred thousand dollars in American money."

Her mouth gaped at the words. "How did he go about collecting that much money for my benefit?"

Dwark told her about the arrival of Lucia Whitfield and the story of the disappearance of the manuscript, that Lucia had learned what had become of it and the payment for it.

He said, "I am going to inform Ling of your father's proposal, but if he shows any sign of treachery, I will have to kill him. You be ready for there may be an uproar in the camp and I'll come for you. Be sure to stay out of the guard's way. He might try to kill you. Otherwise, I will come to report what Ling has said!"

"You cannot do this, Nath," she whispered, clinging to him. "Do nothing that will harm you. You are all that I have left. Please do as I ask!"

Putting both hands on her shoulders he looked deeply into her dark eyes. "I will give my life for you if necessary, Amiya," he said hoarsely. "Now do as I ask. Return to your cabin and wait. I might have to come for you in a hurry!"

With that he walked off hurriedly toward the steep grade where the large cottage sat under a large pine tree. Lights gleamed from the windows giving off a cheerful glow in the mountain darkness. He made a final inspection of his weapons, knocked, then went inside.

"I see that you have come again, Nath Dwark," the man said. He was sitting at the table with a chess board and another player. "What is on your mind this time?" Something about that moon-faced wench?"

Dwark swallowed his wrath. "Bhola Lal Ghosh came to my office today, in Srinagar," he said. "The man has been lucky. He has received money for that manuscript which you demanded from him. He is willing to give it to you provided the girl is returned safely. But you must first deliver her into his hands and he would pay you."

"How much?" Ling asked flatly.

"One hundred thousand dollars in American money."

The Chinaman's eyes blinked slowly behind the blue cigar smoke. Finally he spoke. "That's not enough, I want the full amount which he got for that scroll. My man in Srinagar tells me that he got a bigger sum, two hundred and fifty thousand American dollars.Tell him to deliver it to me here on Thursday of next week, and I will consider letting his daughter leave."

Dwark's temples pounded with thick blood beating against them. After a long time he said, "Consider. You would have to send the girl first!"

"No." Ling lashed out. "I will give the girl back after I'm through with this job."

The impact of his rage struck Dwark's brain so swiftly that his actions were mechanical. Jerking a revolver from his cummerbund he shot the Red agent through the head, then wheeled and fired at those rushing through a side door.

He tried to get out the front window but found it stuck. A bullet pierced his back and the pain jerked him upward out of his precarious position. He leaped out the door, down the steps and ran into the darkness not aware of the gaping wound in his back.

Shortly, he burst into the cabin where Amiya stood pale and trembling. "Come!" he shouted, "We've got to leave. My stallion's up the trail in the brush. You get there while I hold them off!"

He got her outside and up the trail, then stood back waiting for Ling's men. It was only a few minutes for they rushed him shooting their weapons wildly. A stinging pain burnt his great breast. His knees buckled and gave way as he went down firing his revolver. He remembered the hard ground and the sound of hoofs of his iron-gray stallion thudding into the night. His final thought was satisfaction for Amiya had escaped.

The little group of devotees seated themselves upon the grassy area of the ashram, in a half-circle. Harvey Dodds glanced at the face of Shyama, then his glance traveled onward to Lucia who had arrived the evening before. She seemed very natural to be there in that soft sunlight. Lucia had come to India to repay the debt owed to the Ghosh family for the loss of the manuscript in America. She had turned over a large sum of money to Lal Ghosh from the City Museum of New York.

The Master came out of his hut, his benign countenance shining like a beaming light as he gazed upon his chelas, and touched his hands together in greeting. His devoted disciple, Jumnaji, came along behind the Master, with his head humbly bowed. The Godman seated himself upon the ground, his eyes twinkling as he looked around at his devotees.

Then he opened his lips and began to speak. "The aim of all religions and of all ancient seers has been to take the Soul, by one means or another, and put its feet upon the path to God, again

"The successful seeker of God is he who, by practice and contemplation, lifts his Soul to the true kingdom, thus freeing It from all bonds, both internal and external, gross, subtle and causal, and thus separates his mind from the physical environment or the world.

"The perfect saints are those who have reached the last stage, or the true Kingdom of God, that which Lai Tsi speaks about in the Shariyat-Ki-Sugmad. Those who only talk of the perfect saints, or read their teachings to others, without practicing them, are only intellectually educated persons.

"All saints who have come in the past have taught that we must start toward the real center, or true Kingdom of God, through the force of our meditations. Yet not all of us reach the final stage where God alone dwells —the One who is the Ocean of Love and Mercy. Some of us stop at the first plane, others at the second. A few reach the third stage. Only the saints get to the fifth, and very, very few into the highest heaven of all heavens. This is the place of the original departure of the soul toward the lower regions. During its downward journey the soul appears to have descended from the intermediate states, and then to the world in which we are now living.

"The Soul must make this journey through the lower creations in order to find Itself and realize that it has all the godly attributes possible. God makes the Soul take this journey for the reason that It will become the perfected atom and able to do Its spiritual duties.

"Jesus' original teachings gave the sound current as its basic precept. He had studied in India, and it is well known that Jesus was in this country for approximately nineteen years. Two of his cardinal principles are those taught by every ECK Master who has come to this earth. They are: First, the vital importance of love, without which there can be neither wisdom nor religion.

Secondly, that the Kingdom of Heaven is truly a place of reality and that it can be found only within man himself.

"He taught that man should not look into the sky for the true kingdom, but within himself. But his message was poorly received, and meagerly understood, even by his own disciples. None in his day was ready for the lofty ideals, such refined perceptions, and wonderful wisdom.

"The least of all was that none could understand the main point in Jesus' teachings. And it was that the Kingdom of Heaven was a present reality to be known and entered into in this life. Now! This moment! It has always been so. Even today among the most enlightened in the world, only a few can grasp this wonderful, beautiful, sublime ideal. They believe their death will take their souls to the heaven of their desire.

"When told you can pierce the dark veil and enter upon that kingdom now, while in full possession of your senses, you hesitate. Most of you have believed in the past that it was simply a theory due to an overwrought imagination. Yet this very thing was the heart and soul of the message of Jesus, as it has always been in the teachings of the saints.

"But here lies the great block of all religions. The followers cannot believe this. That is why it is emphasized so much about faith. 'If we have the faith of a mustard seed, verily I say unto you whosoever shall say unto this mountain, be thou removed . . .'

"But man cannot understand how we shall enter into the Kingdom of God while in the body. Only the saints offered the definite methods, point to an exact path by which the Kingdom may now be entered. It is no theory but a vital experience that you are given.

"The ECK Masters taught that the great Kingdom was within. They taught the Way, which is the same as the Chinese call the Tao, or what we call the Way of ECKANKAR. No one could grasp it. Yet he insisted that the divine Logos, the Word, was the prime factor in all creation, but it did not register with them.

"And because he taught as one having authority it only insulted the multitude and created anger against himself.

"I am teaching only what others have taught the world. Go read and study your Holy Books and come back tomorrow. Baraka Bashad, may the blessings be!"

They rose from the ground and left, but Harvey Dodds hesitated and the Master turned to him giving the American a keen glance from half-closed eyes.

"You wish to speak with me?" he asked softly.

Dodds said slowly, "Yes, Master. Would it be possible for me to receive the initiation?"

A brilliant smile crossed the Master's bearded face. "I will give you the initiation. Yes, but have patience. It must be at the proper time," he added. "You have seen the great Rebazar Tarzs! I know this by the beauty one radiates after meeting this great Master."

He turned and went into the hut. Dobbs rubbed the light perspiration from his cheek wondering why he had asked that question. Looking up he saw Lucia watching him with shining eyes.

CHAPTER 12

Harvey Dodds was somewhat bothered about Lucia's sudden appearance at the ashram. He kept fighting his attitude well aware that the Master knew perfectly well what was in his heart.

It must have shown in his face for that day the Master talked about self control. Just the same Dodds felt that it would be best to reveal his feelings to Lucia and learn for himself how to get rid of that selfishness within his heart.

After the talk this particular morning Dodds asked the girl if she would walk around the Ashram grounds that afternoon. She said that there was work to be done for the Master but she would do so anyway. The Godman never let any of his chelas stay at the ashram without working at some duty.

Dodds had charge of the medical units and there was always something to do as the villagers arrived daily at the Ashram for supplies during the seasons when food was scarce. When they discovered that the Ashram had a medical service it wasn't long before they were swarming into the yard; the aged, wounded and the injured, old, young, middle-aged women, men and children.

Harvey Dodds went to the women's quarters that afternoon and found Lucia scrubbing the floors. He helped her finish and then they went for a walk along the edge of the steep cliff which ended near a river that gushed over the side in a long waterfall.

"Seems funny that we are doing this sort of thing," he said.

"My friends already think that I am crazy," Lucia replied. "In fact, I think that if I'd go back to New York, they might try to lock me up."

He faced her. "Lucia, I have been thinking about this business of us, both, being here. It seems that I ought to leave."

"You still don't like me, Harvey? Is it because of R. J's treatment of you?"

He nodded. "In spite of the fact that my father did make that mistake and kill your mother, it isn't easy for me to forget what R. J. did. He put my father out of business and tried to do the same to me. And then after learning the truth it was hard to tell you."

"The whole thing is silly. It's in the past so let's forget it. And I think it's all right if we both want to stay here. The trip back to India hasn't been pleasant for me either. I had to face the Ghosh family who believed that my father stole that parchment from Shyama.

"Besides things aren't going well for me. I'm not feeling good and the heavy work I must do here doesn't agree with me. However, I am determined to prove that I'm neither snobbish nor a stuffed shirt because R. J. left me a lot of money!"

She seated herself on a stone wall with

her back to that awful gulf. The valley lay far below them and off into the distance in the misty afternoon sunlight, small rooftops pushed out of the tree tops in gleaming array.

"The Master doesn't want my money," she said in a hurt voice. "I offered all of it to him. He said there were things in America to use it for. Mainly, to build a hospital in Four Rivers for those people who can't pay for regular treatment, including the employees at the plant.

"He explained that Julie Vanners' death served the purpose of showing Four Rivers how badly it needed a hospital. That her karma was served out to help the many, not the few. He says that it wasn't an accident that things have happened as they have, but the play of the divine hand to get the benefit of the money for humanity, instead of a selfish purpose. It is ironic that Father's earnings are serving a cause which he absolutely refused to have anything to do with."

Dodds said curiously, "Why didn't the Master want any of your money?"

"Oh, he took a few dollars. I made arrangements to give him five thousand dollars annually for the next five years. He said that was all he needed. He has to build a new kitchen and stock up on supplies. Has he told you why you were brought back here?"

Dodds shook his head. "Only to help in getting Shyama's sister released from the Reds. He said that now that I was here that she would soon be returning home. I don't know what he meant by that."

Amiya heard the shots at the bungalow and jumped to her feet blowing out the light. She tiptoed to the door and stood listening for the guard. No sound came to her ears except for the wind rustling the leaves of the trees outside.

There was a deadly silence, a silence beyond the conception of thought; one that was pregnant with danger and fear. Her body trembled with anticipation of meeting with the guard.

She searched her mind for some sort of weapon that might protect her against the guard, then remembered the stick of wood left from yesterday's fire. Then she moved cautiously across to the stove and felt in the pitch darkness and found the stovewood.

Slowly, she moved back to the door again and stood waiting. Now the rasping breath of the guard, outside, could be heard. She raised the stick with both hands.

There was a slight scuffling of feet upon the earth and a faint rattle of the door, then it began to push back slowly. A dark shape pushed into the room. She brought the stick down upon the head with all her strength and the guard crumbled without a sound.

She leaned over him listening to his breathing, and satisfied herself that he was not dead, only unconscious. Dropping the club she ran outside and up the trail to where the iron-gray was tied in the brush. The horse snorted slightly as she came out of the darkness and put her hand over its nose.

The sounds of the fight grew closer to the cabin. Wild outcries from the hillmen broke the night, and occasionally Nath Dwark answered them with his great, hoarse shout. Her heart was pounding in her throat as she peered through the brush hoping that the light from the rising moon would show what was happening. Then suddenly the sounds stopped, leaving her as though hung in a world of black space without any visible support.

Cautiously, she peered through the brush again and saw lights flaring from brand-torches coming up the trail. Fear drove through her and quickly mounting the stallion she dug both heels into its flanks. The stallion reared abruptly and neighed wildly breaking into a dead run down the trail in the opposite direction. She seemed to hear Nath Dwark's outcry for her to go, go quickly as possible. She was aware that it was his death cry and stifled the burst of pain in her throat with deep sobbing.

For a long time she let the mount have its way racing through the night, knowing that the Communists would soon be after her. But she had the advantage of the night on her side, for none would dare to race their horses dangerously through the night along a mountain trail as she was doing. She took great chances but cared little about the dangers confronting her.

Almost an hour passed before the valiant stallion began to break its speed and slowly moved into a walk, panting hard. Foam flecked its glossy coat and the perspiration made Amiya have a great sympathy for its efforts to save her from death.

She thought back there in the dark lay her only love, Nath Dwark, a rough bandit chieftain who had given his life for her and sent her home again. She was dry-eyed but deep waves of pain shot through her body.

The first rays of dawn were breaking over the mountains when she became aware of herself again. Then an idea struck her. She could not go back to her father's house in Srinagar for the Reds were surely watching the trail toward the city. She had to go somewhere else and hide until the trouble had passed. Not even her father should know where she went because the Reds might force him into making her return to them.

Then she thought of the Master and decided to go to the Ashram even though it was hundreds of miles from there and she was without a single rupee. Dismounting she let the horse drink from a stream of water flowing through a mountain field. There was nothing else to do but ride that stallion through to the ashram. That was the only way to reach the Master.

Amiya's arrival at the ashram brought great excitement. Rosha and two of the old bandit's gang were caught by the Indian Secret Service and confessed that Ling was dead and the power of the subversive group in northwest India was over. Harvey Dodds was no longer hunted by the reds, and free to move about as desired.

All was soon forgotten in the busy life at the Ashram and Amiya who was ragged, tired and filled with misery over the turn of events which cost the life of her friend, Dwark, turned her mind to her family. She had talked with Shyama and learned that her father was in absolute dejection because of her long absence and now that she was safe was talking with neighbors about her childhood betrothal to a boy, her age, for marriage.

Shyama told her that Lal Ghosh had promised to go through with the marriage provided Amiya was ever released from her captives. Now the day for the wedding date was only a matter of months.

She talked this over with the Master and was told to follow out her father's desire for that was the destiny with which she was to fulfill during her life here. She was aware that in spite of any protest and show of independence that she would have to go through with the plan that her father had made. For an Indian girl to violate the wishes of her family was indeed sacreligious. She was filled with the memories of Nath Dwark and his wonderful love for her. To marry somebody else now was only to diminish her feeling of affection for the dead beloved. She could not even bear to think of this.

She made up her mind to see the American, Harvey Dodds, and talk with him about this. He would understand and perhaps help her in some way. It was only a chance that perhaps something could be done for her that despite the Master's advice could be worked out in harmony for all concerned.

Her love for Nath Dwark would live forever in her memory and never be replaced by anything else. She was aware that the American, Harvey Dodds, would be too gallant to do anything not of the highest order in trying to help her. If only there were some way for her to get to America, then the trouble, and her marriage with her father's choice would not be forced upon her.

What puzzled her, and hurt her consciousness, was that fact that she might completely disobey the Master's advice. She knew that if this were done it would go opposite the divine will. This would make her a disgrace in the eyes of her people and become an outcast among them. This was the worst thing a Hindu girl could do.

However, if she got to America, Shyama could return. Perhaps it would be well that she be able to continue her schooling and with Shyama, return someday to India to help the poor people there.

She knew that if she should make a plan and it got back to her father she might be called there quickly to explain, or he might come to Kumur and take her back to Srinagar. Strangely, he and her mother had not come yet, but seemingly expected that she would be well cared for by the Master who would in time send her home well, again.

Late that afternoon she had the opportunity while alone with Harvey Dodds for a few minutes, to ask if she could see him. She started to ask him if she could have an interview with him late that afternoon or evening, but to her surprise the American proposed that he call upon her shortly and take her for a walk along the river path together.

He told her that he had things to talk over with her.

She promised to meet him by the far corner of the stone fence in the pathway, half the distance toward the river. With a pounding heart she slipped away from the women's quarters without seeing anybody and hurried toward the rendezvous, shortly after dinner. Dodds arrived and greeted her with seeming joy and together they walked toward the river. She was half-guessing what he had to say to her.

It was his farewell to her. Within a few days she had to go home to Srinagar to make preparations for the wedding. He would see the Godman who would give him the answer to his question, which he had come to India to learn and where this would lead him, nobody but the Master knew.

They reached the edge of the water and sat down on the grass listening to the gentle murmuring of the river which flowed down the mountains to the Holy Ganges and then into the sea.

Finally he spoke. "I have heard about what happened to you while you were a prisoner in the mountains. It was God's hand that Nath Dwark did what he did for you!"

"I loved him," she murmured. "But now he is gone; I have nobody to turn to. He was really the first man I have ever loved!"

"I have also heard about your wedding plans, Amiya. I hope that it will be successful and help you get over this memory of Nath Dwark!"

She turned her black eyes upon him. They were filled with a sad light and burned so fiercely that he knew what was behind that wonderful glow.

She said, "I wish it were so. My father made the arrangements when I was a child. I must respect his wishes completely. But I want to change my plans and come to America with you and Shyama."

"You would disobey and come to America with me?" he asked, smiling at her seriousness, trying to turn it off as a jest.

"Yes," she said sadly. "It is in complete disagreement with father's wishes and the Master's advice. My duty, says the Master, is that of obeying God and secondly of following out my responsibility to my family and their wishes."

She continued, "I know that father needs

me badly and that it will hurt him for me to do this. I am not asking that you marry me, or even hinting at such a thing. You must marry Miss Whitfield. She loves you dearly. However, I do not think it is right to marry the man of my father's choice but could put this off by going to America to study in one of the colleges there and returning. By that time I would have my freedom to make my own choice in life."

He said, "I do not know what is right. If the Master will accept me as one of his chelas I will have to stay here and live in the ashram.

"You cannot do that, Harvey. It is not good for you. You Americans need activity and movement. You are too restless. You would die in an ashram."

He shook his head. "Perhaps, but I do not believe that it is true. Anyway, I must refuse your desire to go back with me, unless Lal Ghosh gives his permission."

"He would never do that," she said sadly.

"I am sure you are right," he replied.

She got up quickly and ran up the path toward the ashram without looking back. Tears flowed down her cheeks in humiliation for the rejection she had received brought only shame.

Dodds awoke the following day disheartened over Amiya's reaction and wished that he could do something about it. When he met her later during the day and tried talking with the girl, she completely avoided him. Her eyes were swollen and had a downcast expression. Instead of the friendly, unassuming Amiya, she had become an unhappy girl.

He wanted to talk with the Master about this but knew that Swarachakraji with all his vast powers already knew about the situation and could very well handle it without discussion. But it would relieve his mind to know what the Godman was thinking.

To his surprise the Master sent for him that afternoon. He left his medical hut wondering what the Godman would have to say. In the first place he should have never tried to see the girl alone. She should have been in bed resting.

The Master met him at the door of his hut in an apparent good humor and they sat down together on a grass mat. The Master started talking at once. "I called you back to India to explain the mission of your life.

"What happened to you in America was foreseen long before you left us. You were not ready for the obstacles which you underwent there."

Dodds nodded.

"Amiya is very ill. She needs medical care badly and I am sending her to the nearest hospital which is in Allahabad. Do not worry about her for this is her karma in life and she must bear it, even to the extent of following out her father's desires to marry the man of his choice.

"I know what happened between you and Amiya last evening. I know about everything that goes on between my disciples anywhere in the world. You will someday learn why I say this!

"Amiya's love for Dwark is still burning within her, and unbalancing her mind temporarily, but it will be all right in time. She will marry this man and live a happy life.

"I tell you this. Love is a magnetism between people. We give and take in this love. A child takes its mother's love and the mother takes the love which is from the husband. This secures the home circle in an aura which is most valuable to the human being.

"Remember this, my son. We thrive upon the love of one another. There is no substitute for the love given off by happiness and affection. Those children who have been given love in their life have a wonderful opportunity to find God.

"Now comes the great question for you. Tell me what is the choice you desire to make in life?"

Harvey Dodds said slowly. "I wish to stay here with you for the rest of my life. And I would also like once more to gaze upon the wonderful countenance of Rebazar Tarzs!"

The old man sat in silence for a long time. Finally he said, "I cannot give you the answer, my son. What is to be will be. I will send you into the mountains to meditate. When you receive your answer return and tell me!"

He spoke again. "Tomorrow at sunrise, dress yourself in a blue robe and take the beggar's bowl. Walk the mountain road until you have come to the end of it in the mountain fastness. There find a place of your choice for the spiritual exercises of ECK. When you receive your answer come and tell me!"

Harvey Dodds arose from his bed long before dawn and prepared to leave. Shyama got up and helped him. He was given a dark, blue robe with a cowl that fitted over his head, a begging bowl and sandals lying on a chair by his bed. His regular clothes had disappeared.

He left the Ashram at sunrise. The gray dawn was breaking in the eastern sky with red, purple and green banners. Dressed in the robe as his only garment, he walked up the dusty, rutted mountain road toward the misty peaks which loomed high against the horizon. They were gradually lighted with golden rays of the dawn shining on their lofty, snow-capped heights.

He wondered at himself walking along a lonely mountain road some six thousand miles from America. A little worm of doubt twisted through his heart. What would he find there in his contemplations in the wilds of the Himalayan peaks?

He had to face the wilderness alone with spiritual courage, regardless of danger from bandits and wild animals. He had only his hands, feet and brain and heart to conquor it. This was like Christ in the wilderness, or Buddha under the famous bo-tree. Suddenly he remembered that the Master had not advised him about provisions. He fought down the panic which threatened to override his heart.

He climbed higher into the foothills looking backwards into the valley where lay the little town of Kumur. It kept growing smaller with each footstep he took upward toward the lofty peaks of the giant range.

Some way beyond the road would run out and he would have to walk among the wild crags searching for a place where he would contemplate for his answer or die of starvation. He had asked Lucia to wait for his return and received her promise.

During the middle of the afternoon Dodds limped into a tiny village that clung perilously to the mountainside. He was surprised to see the villagers were expecting him, and one who could speak English said that word had been received about him. He wondered but was too tired to ask questions. The villagers fed him and let him sleep for a couple of hours, then the one who spoke English took him to a small temple where dwelled the Holy Man of the village.

The Holy Man was an old, old person who was seated in a lotus posture upon a tiger skin. He looked straight ahead into infinity. The villager acted as an interpreter. After a long time the old man replied in a low humming voice that sung with joy.

The man said, "Our Holy Man says you

must sit here with him. He says that you must spend the night here in prayer and continue your journey tomorrow. He says that you will meet with great experience in the mountains."

"I will follow his wishes," Harvey Dodds replied.

They sat together, the three of them, nothing said, and the strange humming sound in the air about them made Dodds curious.

After what seemed to be eternity to Dodds the old man spoke again to the villager. The man got up and motioned for Dodds to follow. They went outside in the darkness. The villager said, "Stay here tonight under the tree and listen for God's voice. You will leave again at sunrise!"

Dodds stayed all night under the tree but did not experience anything. The next morning he ate and took up his journey again toward the high peaks. The wild range seemed to stand up straight, sparkling clean and white in the sunlight.

The day passed and the sun became a great ball of orange fire in the west when he came to the end of the little road. It ran out into a trail lost in the gray, ugly landscape fit only for the grazing of sheep.

The slope worked out flat from the trail and before him were several large rocks. A lone cedar tree stood nearby in the desolate area. He decided it needed him as much as he needed its company, and went over to take a seat crosslegged under its sparse branches.

He closed his eyes and let his thoughts

dwell upon the light within himself. He did not know how long he sat in silence but gradually became aware that time was passing.

The night moved by and his body became weary, but stubbornly he held to his task. Something began to happen within him and then a quietness stole over his mind. Some far off music, the strange sound of a high rising wind becoming stronger, was moving into his consciousness.

He opened his eyes. At first he thought the shining gray light was from the dawn. Then realized it was too early for daybreak. Then he perceived it was a bright nothingness, increasing until it grew into a blinding yellow light beyond all conception. All at once its brightness took on every hue of the rainbow and he realized that he was observing and experiencing something beyond his wildest imagination. He was drowning in a sea of roaring sounds.

The light suddenly cleared and before him stood a shining figure of a youth with the most beautiful eyes that Dodds had ever seen in anyone. On the forehead was painted the grilled insignia of the Lord of the World.

A melodious voice seemed to speak from everywhere. "I am Viswapati, Lord of the Universe. I am here because you have called for me to give you the enlightenment of yourself, O man of the earth realm!

"You come to the mountains seeking me. Only I can give you the true answer to all life!

"The answer to all things is within you. You must find me within your heart and every answer to life's obstacles will be realized.

"This night you have looked into your heart and found me there. Your answer is this. Return to your country, and the little town where you have had so much difficulty. There you must practice the arts of healing again. This is your destiny—to help mankind through the art of healing. Take the Indian boy with you and see that he gets the proper training to become a great physician to help his own people.

"Take the American girl in marriage. It is the destiny of your life, for you both, and you have been together before throughout the centuries in other incarnations. Your path will be made easier once you have taken the initiation through the Master."

"Lord," Dodds said. "Have I the strength to carry out this mission?"

A beautiful smile lighted the being's countenance. "Fear not for strength for my presence will be with you always. I have been with you through the centuries. I was with you in Korea, during the months of your imprisonment, and while you marched over the mountains into Kashmir. I was the man on the road to Kumur. I stood at your side when you addressed the group of Americans on the art of ECK. I was Rebazar Tarzs in the California mountains. I was the one who appeared to those who came to help you escape from India. I am Swarachakraji, the Wheel of Heaven, and I am Soul in you, the Mahanta, the Living ECK Master.

"As you work to help mankind you must also teach and practice the art of divine love for all. You will become my missionary in America. Thousands will flock to you to learn the secret of this ancient art.

"I am everywhere. I am in everything. I know all things. You cannot live without me, and above all love me completely for I am the Lord of the Worlds.

"Worship me with a flower, a leaf, a fruit, or a stone, but worship me. I am every avatar and saint in the world.

"I come whenever man needs me. When the world becomes filled with strife and no longer can man control the elements of trouble, I appear again as the Godman to show him the way to peace and happiness.

"Be of pure heart when you worship me for I am the inspiration and the ideal of the life of your Soul. I am the supreme, eternal reality of all the ever changing worlds, and the friend of all things. If you know me thus you shall attain peace.

"I will say goodbye but not farewell for we shall meet again, many times. Repeat my name often for he who does so receives a spiritual blessing each time. When you need me, call and I will come."

The shining figure faded gently away into the gray of dawn leaving Dodds breathlessly rooted to the earth.

Long afterwards when the sunlight first filled the mountain tops, Harvey Dodds arose from his position under the lonely cedar and walked lightly over the earth as if he expected it to open and swallow him. He reached the village, passed through and got to the ashram late that afternoon and fell on his face at the Master's door.

He was put on a cot in the medical quarters and Shyama left with him. He was given a sleeping drug by the doctor and slept soundly.

When he awoke the sunlight was filling the little hut. He realized that he had slept through the night into the following morning. Shyama was seated at the foot of the bed, half-asleep, from his long night's vigil. He opened his eyes and looked at Harvey Dodds.

"You have rested well, my elder brother," he said quietly. "She is here to see you!"

Turning his head he found Lucia standing by the bed looking like a lovely angel, her hair shining in the light. Smiling, she said, "You cannot do anything about this now. You're helpless."

"I'm glad," he whispered, reaching for her hand. He looked at her with his eyes shining in tears. "I've been a fool, Lucia. We could have been happy a long time ago if I'd known the truth."

She put a finger on his lips. "We will talk later," she murmured.

She stood back as the Master entered

the door with a wonderful smile. Dodds instantly realized how much the old man looked like the youth in the mountains. Could it be possible they were the same person?

The Master said, "I am happy over your decision to return to America. If you can be ready at high noon today I will give you and Lucia the initiation for ECKANKAR."

Dodds looked at Lucia knowing he had not asked her to marry him, but saw the smile on her face. He took her hand and turned back to the Master.

"We would like to be married," he said in a husky voice.

Radiant joy seemed to fill the Master's face. He murmured, "Your initiation will be your marriage vows. Afterward you may go to the Church of your faith in the city and repeat your vows for the sake of your western customs."

The initiation was given at high noon in the little chapel on the ashram grounds. Afterwards Dodds and the girl went to a church in the city where a Scottish minister married them according to the Christian faith.

When the plane rose in the air the next morning from Kumur, he and Lucia were sitting together. Across the aisle watching them was Shyama, but Harvey Dodds and Lucia were looking through the window at the little city on the earth below. They could make out the buildings of the ashram which he nor Lucia were ever to see again. The dream of those beautiful days there hurried through his mind.

He thought of Amiya and her father, the flight across India to escape the Reds; of his escape from China and the old Kazakhs' chief, Batir, now dead; and his followers scattered in the mountains of Kashmir. And of the beauty of the light and sound of Viswapati among the wild mountain crags in the early dawn.

Then he suddenly knew the beauty of Swarachakraji and the strength of Rebazar Tarzs. They were so much like Viswapati. How could they be different? Why there was no difference at all. They were the same person, the same Soul.

"Swarachakraji is Viswapati," he said suddenly looking at Shyama. "And Viswapati is Swarachakraji. The Wheel of Heaven is the Lord of the World, and Rebazar Tarzs is each of them!"

"Yes, my brother," softly came Shyama's voice. "That is the truth. At last you know the secret of everything."

His hand closed slowly over Lucia's fingers. She smiled gently at him with a great light in her eyes. He spoke again, half to himself. "Then I am the Master, and the Master is me."

The boy whispered back. "You have discovered the true secret of the universe, my brother!"

Joy burst through him as the plane sped through the soft white clouds over the ancient land of India. He knew now that Viswapati, the Lord of the World, was the Soul of God, and himself.

ECKANKAR Presents a Spiritual Study Course: *Soul Travel—The Illuminated Way*

People want to know the secrets of life and death. In response to this need Paul Twitchell, the modern-day founder of ECKANKAR, brought to light the Spiritual Exercises of ECK—which offer a direct way to God.

Those who are ready to begin a study of ECKANKAR can receive special monthly discourses which give clear, simple instructions for these exercises. The first twelve-month series is called *Soul Travel—The Illuminated Way*. Mailed each month, the discourses are designed to lead the individual to the Light and Sound of God.

The techniques in these discourses, when practiced twenty minutes a day, are likely to prove survival beyond death. Many have used them as a direct route to Self-Realization, where one learns his mission in life. The next stage, God Consciousness, is the joyful state wherein Soul becomes the spiritual traveler, an agent for God. The underlying principle one learns then is this: "Soul exists because God loves It."

Discourses include these titles, among others: "The Universality of Soul Travel," "The Illuminated Way by Direct Projection," and "The Spiritual Cities of This World." These can be studied at home or with fellow students in a local ECKANKAR class—look in the phone book under ECKANKAR, or write us for classes in your area.

For more information on how to receive *Soul Travel—The Illuminated Way* and ECKANKAR classes in your area, use the coupon at the back of this book, or write:

ECKANKAR, P.O. Box 3100, Menlo Park, CA 94026 U.S.A.

Introductory Books on ECKANKAR
The Ancient Science of Soul Travel

The Wind of Change, Sri Harold Klemp

What are the hidden spiritual reasons behind every event in your life? With stories drawn from his own life-long training, ECKANKAR's spiritual leader shows you how to use the power of Spirit to discover those reasons. Follow him from the Wisconsin farm of his youth, to a military base in Japan; from a job in Texas, into the realms beyond, as he shares the secrets of ECKANKAR.

In My Soul I Am Free, Brad Steiger

Here is the incredible life story of Paul Twitchell—prophet, healer, Soul Traveler—whose spiritual exercises have helped thousands to contact the Light and Sound of God. Brad Steiger lets the famed ECK Master tell you in his own words about Soul Travel, healing in the Soul body, the role of dreams and sleep, and more. Includes a spiritual exercise called "The Easy Way."

ECKANKAR—The Key to Secret Worlds, Paul Twitchell

Paul Twitchell, modern-day founder of ECKANKAR, gives you the basics of this ancient teaching. Includes six specific Soul Travel exercises to see the Light and hear the Sound of God, plus case histories of Soul Travel. Learn to recognize yourself as Soul—and journey into the heavens of the Far Country.

The Tiger's Fang, Paul Twitchell

Paul Twitchell's teacher, Rebazar Tarzs, takes him on a journey through vast worlds of Light and Sound, to sit at the feet of the spiritual Masters. Their conversations bring out the secret of how to draw closer to God—and awaken Soul to Its spiritual destiny. Many have used this book, with its vivid descriptions of heavenly worlds and citizens, to begin their own spiritual adventures.

For more free information about the books and teachings of ECKANKAR, please write: **ECKANKAR, P.O. Box 3100, Menlo Park, CA 94026 U.S.A.**

Or look under ECKANKAR in your local phone book for an ECKANKAR Center near you.